# ICE DANCING

**Look for more of
Alex and Samantha's adventures in:**

*Ice Princess*

# ICE DANCING

## Nicholas Walker

AN
**APPLE**
PAPERBACK

SCHOLASTIC INC.
New York Toronto London Auckland Sydney

ISBN 0-590-46764-6

12 11 10 9 8 7 6 5 4 3 2 1          4 5 6 7 8 9/9

Printed in the U.S.A.          40

First Scholastic printing, January 1994

*My thanks go to Rosalind Newman
for help with the research.*

*This book is dedicated to my daughter JAIME,
always my greatest fan.*

# Contents

# 1.
# Parting of the Ways

Alex gazed across the endless expanse of the huge ice rink and wondered if he was going to be sick. The judges didn't seem in any hurry; they were still fussing around, discussing the last two skaters.

"What's wrong with you?" demanded his partner, Diane.

"Nothing," he said. "I just wish they'd get a move on."

"Well, try and stay on your feet, will you?" she said in a bitter voice. "You nearly made me fall the last time." It wasn't true, but Alex didn't say anything. Diane was always looking for a fight.

This was the first time they had skated a medal test together. Diane's run-through had gone well but now the judges had turned their attention to Alex and all his confidence had oozed away.

At last, the middle judge leaned towards the microphone on the table in front of him.

"Alex Barnes, foxtrot," he said, making Alex

jump. He skated out onto the ice. Diane deliberately made him wait alone out there, while she tucked her lace inside her boot. Finally, she was ready and they took up their starting positions.

*Bang!* Their music started, sounding tinny in the empty auditorium. One, two, three, the music played until on the fourth bar they moved with it. Alex's feet automatically followed the tempo though his mind was still in pieces. For the first circuit things went quite well but, as they passed the judges' table, he started to shake.

His timing was off and the end barrier was coming up fast. He changed from one edge of his skate to the other but he was running out of ice and Diane was already doing their turn.

"Wait," he said, almost desperately.

"*You're* too slow!" she shot back.

He made a face and then remembered the judges were looking at him. Clutching Diane's hand he tried to make her go a little wider but she just stuck remorselessly to the routine. They circled the far end again and Alex's skate got away from him. He grabbed for Diane to stay on his feet. She helped, but not much. Then it was the final circuit and their routine took them to a halt in front of the judges. Diane curtsied and Alex gave his formal bow, and they skated off, almost running away.

Liz Pope, the junior dance team coach, was

waiting for them. She had a serious look on her face.

"Well, yours went OK, Diane," she said.

"No thanks to this jerk!" snapped Diane. "His timing's been off all morning — if he's lost me my medal . . ."

"The only one who's lost a medal is me," said Alex crossly, "so do me a favor and shut up, will you?"

"Shut up yourself!" retorted Diane.

"Stop it, Diane," said Liz. "You could've helped, you know, especially on that last circuit."

"If he can't cut it I don't see why I should carry him."

"Because you're partners," said Liz crossly.

"If he wants to stay my partner he's going to have to get his act together!"

Liz looked as if she was about to make an angry retort, but at the last moment, she thought better of it and turned back to Alex. "Look, you're on again in a minute for your solo. They're bound to ask you to repeat your foxtrot so you've got a chance to show them you can do it properly."

"What's the point? I've got to score at least 2.8 for each dance. There's no way I'm anywhere near that on the foxtrot alone," said Alex. "I might as well quit now."

"Don't you dare! You go out there and do the best you can," said Liz. "I know they're not supposed to mark the solo but it can make all the difference."

Alex sighed and trooped back onto the ice. Sure enough they asked him to repeat his foxtrot, but he knew he'd already blown it so he just went through the motions. He came back and sat on the opposite end of the bench to Diane. Liz didn't say anything but she had an exasperated look on her face. The last two skaters went on and Liz went over to the judges' table to hear the verdict. She seemed to be gone for ages. When she came back she looked at Alex and shook her head.

"Sorry Alex," she said.

"Not your fault, Liz," he said. "Was I the only one who struck out?"

"Yes, we were lucky. Don't worry, you'll get it the next time." She turned to Diane. "Well done, Diane."

"Yes, congrats," said Alex.

"And I've got to go on practicing all the beginner's stuff for another four months waiting for you!" Diane said testily.

"No you don't," said Alex getting to his feet. "I'll save you the trouble. Go find yourself a partner who can keep up with you."

"What? You're walking out on me?" Diane demanded. "You — " She broke off, lost for words. "You're not busting up this partnership, Alex Barnes — I am! There's no way I'd ever skate with you again!"

4

"Anything you say, Diane," said Alex levelly. He stepped back onto the ice and glided across to congratulate the other skaters.

"Good riddance!" Diane shouted after him. Liz waited until he was out of earshot before speaking.

"You are an idiot, Diane. You've been working on that partnership for over six months!"

"Oh, he's useless, Liz. I'm never going to get anywhere carrying him around."

"Alex is an excellent skater! You've been skating years longer than he has and you only had to help a bit," said Liz. She strode off across the ice, her boots making a crackling sound on the frozen surface.

When she caught up with him, Alex was sitting on the bench outside the changing room, unlacing his skates.

"Alex?"

"Oh, hi Liz. Sorry I left a bit suddenly," he said.

"That's all right, I know you're feeling a bit upset," she said. "Look, are you serious about not skating with Diane?"

"Yes."

"Just because you failed a medal test?"

"It's nothing to do with the test," he said. "Oh, sure, I'm fed up with failing. But I almost expected to fail. It's never really worked with Diane."

"You just need a bit more practice, that's all."

5

"Yeah, if it was just the skating that was wrong I'd believe you, but you can't practice liking each other," he said. "I'll tell you straight, Liz, I've tried to like Diane, but it's no use." He slid off his second skate and stood up. "And without that, it's never going to work, is it?"

She shook her head. "No, Alex, it's never going to work."

He grinned. "Better the way it is then."

"You're not thinking of giving up, are you?"

"I dunno. I mean I'll never quit skating but I don't know about competing anymore. I might concentrate more on my hockey. I don't have to take medals for that," he said. "Anyway, thanks for your help, Liz. You did your best." He leaned forward and gave her a kiss on the cheek. "C'mon, don't look so fed up, it's me that's failed."

She gazed after him, as he disappeared into the changing room.

"No, it's not," she said quietly to herself.

# 2.
# The New Girl

Alex Barnes was fourteen and already the tallest boy in his class. He was slim, with dark hair that was always untidy. Alex was what his sports teacher called a natural born athlete. He threw himself into most school sports, as well as skating three nights a week at the local ice rink. The only problem with Alex was that for him, sports were just games, and he refused to take them too seriously.

Alex was in the eighth grade at Mount's Park School. When he strolled into registration on Monday morning, his best friend Toby was waiting eagerly for him. Theirs was an unlikely friendship, because Toby's main interest in life was food: eating it, cooking it, thinking about it, even dreaming about it. Toby's ambition was to be a chef and the thought of any physical activity other than cooking made him break out in a cold sweat. In spite of this he was Alex's most devoted supporter.

Ice dancing was Toby's least favorite sport but he still came hurrying over.

"Well?" he demanded.

"Well what?" Alex said, taken aback.

"Did you pass?" He looked at Alex's baffled stare: "The medal test, balloon brain!"

"Oh that — no, no I didn't," said Alex. "I messed up the foxtrot."

"Oh." Toby's face fell. He was considerably more upset about it than Alex was. His friend grinned at his expression.

"Don't worry Toby, I can take it again."

"What did Diane say?"

"What didn't she say!" said Alex. "We've decided we can struggle through life without one another."

"But how are you going to manage without a partner?" Toby demanded. "You're not going to give up, are you?" Alex didn't have the heart to say he'd been thinking about it.

"I can skate on my own for a while," he said evasively.

"You should've let me come to cheer you on."

"You don't cheer people on at a medal test . . ." Alex broke off as a girl he hadn't seen before pushed unceremoniously past him. "Who's that?" he demanded.

"Oh yes, I'd forgotten. You were goofing off on that geography field trip last week, weren't you?" said Toby. "She started Wednesday. She's from some posh boarding school in Edinburgh."

"I wasn't goofing off," said Alex, watching as

8

the new girl sat down at a lonely desk in the front row. "We were collecting rock samples."

"Oh yeah? And how many did you bring back?"

Alex ignored him.

"Anyway, I don't think they should put all the new people in with us. Why can't they stick them in another homeroom?" said Toby.

"What's she like?"

"Dunno, she never speaks."

"Probably shy."

"Nah — she's just a snob."

"She could be a bit lonely," said Alex. "I wonder if I should go and have a chat."

"You mean, will she go out with you?"

"Of course I do."

"Well, the answer's no, she won't!"

"D'you want to put money on it?"

"How much?" said Toby so quickly Alex should have suspected something, but he was still looking at the new girl.

"A dollar?"

"You're on," said Toby. "How long do you want?"

"Eh — oh, I dunno, how about a week?" said Alex.

"You can have two if you like," said Toby. Alex turned to look at him.

"You're being very fair," he said. "What aren't you telling me?"

"Nothing, it's just that Phil Price moved in on Thursday and got turned down flat, and when Steve Hoskin from the ninth grade asked her to the school dance she told him to get lost!"

"Ah," said Alex. "We haven't actually made that bet, have we?"

"Yes," grinned Toby.

"Well, here goes nothing," said Alex. "I think I'll go and borrow her math homework."

"You won't, Hurricane's just arrived," said Toby. "C'mon, let's get a desk at the back."

Fifty minutes later when Mr. Higgins, the geography teacher, was drawing a map on the board, the two boys were playing cards under the desk. Mr. Higgins was as far from his nickname "Hurricane" as he could be. He was an easy-going, but boring, teacher and his students were quite happy to let him get on with drawing his map if he left them alone. All in all it was a fairly typical geography lesson: Roberta Isgrove was painting her nails, Jennie Mulliner was writing a letter to her pen-pal in Australia, David Biggs was doing his math homework, Mike Harvey was shooting rubber bands at Paula Tomkins who knew she was perfectly safe as long as he was actually aiming them at her, while Phil Price had his eyes closed. Of the rest of the class only five were actually working while the others were giving a very good impression.

Mr. Higgins turned around suddenly and saw what seemed to be a peaceful class, except for Toby and Alex who were having an argument about the last deal. Mr. Higgins reached for the eraser and hurled it across the room. Alex, who fielded for the school baseball team, plucked it out of the air.

"Howzat?" he cried.

"Out — and back to the pavilion," said Mr. Higgins. He pointed to the empty chair by the new girl. "Here, Barnes, where I can keep an eye on you." Alex made a face but he was secretly pleased, seeing a chance to win the dollar off Toby. He gathered up his books and plonked himself down at the front desk.

Alex looked at the new girl. "I don't suppose you play blackjack, do you?" he said.

"What?" The voice was a snap.

"Forget it," said Alex. She gave a shrug and went back to the book in front of her. Alex sneaked a glance, thinking she'd be one of the few actually working, but she was drawing a line of figures wearing leotards.

"They told me you didn't speak," he said. She acted as though she hadn't heard and Alex nearly gave up but could always use a little money.

"My name's Alex Barnes," he said, but she obviously didn't care. There was a long silence, then, "You're supposed to tell me your name now, that's

11

how it works," he said. She turned her eyes on him.

"Will it shut you up if I do?" she demanded.

"Oh, I doubt it," he grinned. "You could give it a try I suppose."

"It's Samantha Stephens — now is that it?"

"There, that didn't hurt, did it?"

"Look," she said, "I'm sure you think that every girl should throw herself at your feet, but leave me out of your silly games, will you?"

"Wow, I think I liked it better when you weren't speaking," said Alex. Rebuffs never worried Alex. He had been asking Roberta Isgrove, the eighth grade Madonna, to go to the monthly school dance with him for over a year and she still kept saying no.

He nudged Samantha and grinned at her expression. "They say you've been going to some posh school in Edinburgh?" he said.

"*They* must be right then."

"Was it one of the famous ones? You know, like the Royal Family go to?"

"It was called the Tracy Powell School of Dance, if it's got anything to do with you."

"That's one of those performing arts schools, isn't it?" he said. "Where they make you work around the clock?" He didn't think she was going to reply.

"Yes," she said almost in a whisper.

"I couldn't put up with all that discipline," he said.

"No."

"I bet you were glad to get away from all that?" he said.

"Darn you! Why don't you just leave me alone!" Alex flinched. She was on her feet, her dark eyes blazing with fury. The whole class froze at the transformation.

"All of you!" she shouted. "Leave me alone!" Then she ran from the room, slamming the door.

Mr. Higgins stood frozen, a piece of chalk still in his hand. At last, he turned his gaze on Alex.

"Don't look at me," said Alex. "I never laid a finger on her."

Mrs. Stephens was making the beds when she heard the back door open. Puzzled, she hurried downstairs to find Samantha slumped in one of the kitchen chairs.

"Hello, darling," said Mrs. Stephens. "What are you doing home?" Samantha didn't reply. Mrs. Stephens sighed and sat down opposite her. "Did you cut school, darling?" she said gently.

"Yes."

"Why?"

"I had an argument with somebody."

"Well now, that's just a part of going to school,

isn't it?" said her mother. "It must have been more than that, surely?"

"He told me that I was lucky not to be going to dance school anymore," said Samantha.

"Ah." Mrs. Stephens was silent for a moment, then, "Well, never mind. You have a nice lunch with me then go back this afternoon."

"We have gym class this afternoon. I'm not allowed to go to gym!"

"You've still got to go, Samantha, you know that," said Mrs. Stephens, getting to her feet. "Now come on, what would you like for lunch? Something special?"

"It's not fair, Mommy," said Samantha, her eyes filling her tears.

"Oh, Samantha, we've been through this hundreds of times," said Mrs. Stephens. "It's nobody's fault. You can't dance anymore and that's all there is to it."

"I've danced every day of my life since I was five years old!" said Samantha.

"I know, darling."

"Do you?" Samantha demanded, getting to her feet. *Do you?* My muscles twitch so much I can't sleep at night. My body aches whenever I'm still, I've got a headache all the time, I can't eat, I can't work — and you won't even let me exercise!" She went over and opened the kitchen door and looked back at her mother. "So, you tell me, what is it

14

you expect me to do?" She slammed the door behind her.

Mrs. Stephens stood looking after her daughter, then sat down at the table again.

"I just want you to learn to be a normal child," she said quietly to herself.

# 3.
# Breaking the Ice

Going out, darling?" Mrs. Stephens' voice came from the living room. It was later the same day and Samantha, who had been trying to sneak out of the front door, gave a sigh.

"Yes, Mommy," she said, putting her head round the door. "I thought I'd go for a walk."

"I hear you had some trouble at school this morning," said Mr. Stephens, putting down his newspaper.

"Yeah, a bit," said Samantha, coming into the room.

"Don't say 'yeah,' darling," said her mother.

"Sorry — I sorted it all out. I went back and apologized to the geography teacher. He was fine about it."

"So how are you doing in school?" asked her father. "Made any friends yet?"

"I've talked to a few people, yes," said Samantha. "They all hang around that arcade on Main Street. I thought I might stop by."

"If it's dark when you come out, you're to get a taxi home," said Mr. Stephens.

"It's hardly more than a mile," said Samantha.

"If you don't, you're not going!" said her father. He reached for his wallet and produced a five dollar bill.

"Er — no thanks, it's OK. I've got money."

"Sure?"

"Yeah — I mean yes. I've still got all this year's tuition fees left." She went and kissed her father. "Don't worry, I'll be all right."

Her parents sat looking at each other until they heard the front door slam.

"You've got to start letting her go out, Donald," said Mrs. Stephens.

"She's only fourteen!"

"Yes, but for the last three years she's been living away from home. She's well able to take care of herself."

Samantha swung aimlessly down the road in the opposite direction to the arcade. She hated Mount's Park School and longed for the close-knit friendship of her last school, where everybody was united by their passion for dance.

For half an hour she walked slowly, enjoying the feeling of exercising, not noticing where she was going. Then suddenly she found herself outside the ice rink. She sat on the low car-park wall, swinging her legs, and wondering if she should go inside. At last, making up her mind, she followed a group of people through the glass doors into the rink.

Samantha gasped. The rink was enormous and packed with people all cheering a furious ice hockey match. Feeling very small and insignificant, she slid into an empty seat in the back row.

Alex was having a bad night! He was the junior hockey team's number one scorer but tonight it just wasn't happening. Finally the puck came his way. He trapped it, turned in a tight circle, and was dumped by his opposite number.

"C'mon ref! Open your eyes!" he heard the huge voice of Chris Macdonald come bellowing across the ice. Alex scrambled up, chased after his opponent, caught him behind the goal and smashed him against the barriers. The referee blew his whistle.

"You!" he pointed at Alex. "Board checking! Two minutes!"

Alex opened his mouth to protest then gave a shrug and skated off to the sidelines.

"It's your own fault!" Chris Macdonald snarled from the bench. "Right in front of the ref, you idiot!" Chris Macdonald was the team coach and was as big as his voice.

"It was only retaliation," protested Alex.

"He didn't even have the puck!" snapped Chris. "Leaving us with five players at this stage of the game! You could've cost us this match!"

"Ah, they're nine points ahead, we'll never

catch them up anyway," said Alex. Chris gave him a fierce look, so Alex hurriedly retreated to the penalty bench.

His two-minute penalty seemed to go on forever but, at last, he was free and he went charging back into the fray. And then, in the final seconds of the game, things went Alex's way. He made one of his fast rushes up the ice, dodged sideways to send the goalkeeper the wrong way, and scored beautifully in the top left corner of the net.

The crowd went wild and he raised his arms in triumph. Almost immediately the referee blew his whistle for the end of the game and Alex let himself glide to the edge, where Toby was sitting in the front row.

"Bad luck," he said.

"Bad luck?" demanded Alex. "How about that for a brilliant goal?"

"Yeah, it was great," agreed Toby. "But I mean you didn't win, did you?"

"Aw, it was only a friendly game."

"There's no such thing," said Toby.

"You take things too seriously," said Alex, helping himself to a handful of Toby's popcorn. "Look, I'd better get changed. There's a dance class as soon as they've resurfaced the ice. You're not staying, are you?"

"No way, not for ice dancing!" Toby said in horror. "Anyway, the pizzeria's open."

Alex grinned. "Well, I can't compete with that,"

he said. "Thanks for coming anyway — see you in the morning."

It took Alex half an hour to change out of his body armor. When he got back to the ice, the dance class was in full swing. Liz saw him and came over.

"Hello Alex, I wasn't sure I'd see you again," she said.

"Neither was I," he admitted. "But my mother would kill me if I gave up after she'd finally bought me some new skates."

"You're still serious about splitting up with Diane though?"

"Oh, I think so. Anyway, she wouldn't touch me with a ten-foot pole after Saturday."

"She would. It's just her pride that's hurt," said Liz. She glanced around at the other skaters. "Trouble is, I've got no one looking for a regular partner at the moment." Alex followed her gaze; though there were twice as many girls as boys skating, most of them were paired up together. Diane was skating with Nigel.

"That's all right, I don't mind skating solo," said Alex.

"But if you're going in for the next Bronze test you should be practicing as a pair."

"Oh, who cares about the tests," said Alex. "Look, I just want to enjoy myself, Liz — OK?"

Liz sighed as he shot off around the ice. Alex could be the best skater there, but he was never going to get anywhere with his attitude. She lined everybody up and took them through some basic steps: chassés, crossrolls, mohawks, and choctaws. Alex had been skating for four years now and the basic steps came easy. The trouble was bothering to get them exactly right. For hockey it didn't matter. He just needed to stay upright and move fast.

Slowly the class moved on to simple dance steps and finally they paired up to go through the dances for the medal tests.

Diane was steadfastly ignoring Alex, who paired up with Sue that evening. Sue was an eighteen-year-old solo skater who came to the classes for extra training, but she was good to dance with because she was so advanced.

"Word's going round that it was *Diane* who dumped *you*," she said to him.

"Yeah?" Alex grinned. "I wonder who started that rumor?"

"What did you expect? Trouble is, Alex, she's telling everybody you nearly cost her her medal."

"And they're listening to that garbage?" said Alex surprised.

"Some of them, yeah," said Sue. "Diane seems very nice, until you really get to know her."

"Yeah, I quite liked her at first," admitted Alex. "You have to remember with Diane, there's a lot less to her than meets the eye."

"She can do you a lot of harm, Alex," said Sue

seriously. "I doubt you'll find another partner at the moment."

"You'd think Liz could do something."

"Oh, c'mon Alex, what do you expect?" said Sue. "If she gets rid of Diane that's the end of the junior dance club. Diane's mother puts the money behind it. She practically owns it."

"And that's what's wrong with it," said Alex.

"Hardly any of the other rinks have a junior dance club," said Sue. "They think you should all do pairs until you are older and strong enough to cut the deep edges you need."

"I know, Sue," said Alex. "Look, don't worry about it. I'm not really looking for another partner."

"Well, I'll always partner you if you're stuck, you know that. But you understand with me it's strictly temporary."

Alex was glad when Liz finally broke the class up. He had had enough after the hockey as well. Besides, he didn't seem particularly popular with the others. Sue was the only one really speaking to him.

He trooped wearily up the steps. Nearly all the spectators had gone when the hockey match finished, and he was surprised to see a familiar face in the back row.

"Oh, hi — er . . . er, Samantha!" he said, remembering her name at the last moment. "What are you doing here?"

"Hang gliding."

He grinned. "Did you see me playing hockey?"

"Is that what that organized brawl was? Yes, I did," she said.

"Did you see my goal?" he said, still not put out. "Was I good, or was I good!"

"I've really no idea, I've never been in a rink before." She gave a shrug. "I just dropped in to pass the time."

"Now that's an excellent reason to come to an ice rink," he said. "Did you like the dance class better then?"

"I understood it more, yes," she said. "I'm not sure I see the point through."

"Well you wouldn't, watching us," he said. "Tell you what, though, if you'd really like to understand it, why don't you come along Saturday night?"

"What's so special about Saturday night?"

"Jayne Torvill and Christopher Dean are giving an exhibition," said Alex. Then, seeing his chance: "I'll get you a ticket if you like."

"I promise I can afford my own ticket," she said, getting to her feet. "That's if I decide to come."

"Oh," he said. He regarded her for a moment. "If you hang around for a couple of minutes I could walk you home."

"I know the way, thank you."

"I was just trying to be friendly," he said. "I could explain all about ice dancing."

"Look — er, Alan, I dropped in because I was bored, and I stayed to watch some ice dancing. I've seen some now and I'm not particularly impressed — and that's it, OK?" She didn't wait for his reply but turned and disappeared through the exit doors. Alex watched her go.

"Alex," he said out loud. "The name's Alex!"

# 4.
# Basic Steps

Diane's mother made sure the dance club got really good seats for Saturday's show. Alex, who was sitting as far away from Diane as he could, was fidgeting around, gazing at the rest of the audience behind him. Toby, in the next seat, looked up and gave him a nudge.

"Sit down, will you?" he said. "You nearly made me drop my ice cream."

"Oh, we can't have that," said Alex, subsiding into his seat.

"Who are you looking for, anyway?"

"Samantha Stephens," said Alex. "I thought she might have come."

"Oh, I'd forgotten about our bet," said Toby. "How are things going?"

"Fine," said Alex. "Absolutely great."

"Yeah?" said Toby. He gazed at Alex, who grinned, felt in his pocket, and handed Toby a dollar.

"Told you," said Toby.

"Yes, and if you tell me again, that ice cream's going down the back of your neck," said Alex.

"I don't know why you bothered in the first place."

"Because of the bet," said Alex. "Then I really did begin to feel sorry for her. But I'll tell you straight, Toby, she's not that easy to like!'

"But you still thought she might be here?"

"She's supposed to be interested in dance, isn't she?"

"Obviously not that interested — not like me," said Toby. He heaved a sigh and glanced at his watch. "How long does this thing go on for?"

"This thing?" Alex demanded.

"Yeah, this dancing thing," said Toby. "It's not too long, is it? I haven't anything else to eat."

Alex regarded him disapprovingly. "You're a peasant, you are," he said.

"Yeah, I know," Toby said. He brightened. "Tell you what, we could get a hot dog at intermission."

The reason Alex couldn't see Samantha was because he was looking in the wrong place. She was sitting in the main box with everybody else who could afford expensive tickets. Samantha's father was very generous with money, especially since he'd taken Samantha away from her dance school.

Samantha wouldn't have missed tonight's show for anything. She was passionately interested in dance, even though to her ice dancing wasn't the real thing. She sat staring out across the ice, feeling slightly superior. Even when the two famous figures appeared and started to skate, she still only watched halfheartedly. Then, gradually, her gaze grew more and more fixed.

There were usually about twenty in the junior dance club, but when Alex came into the main ring on Monday night, the ice was packed. He sighed. That was the trouble. Whenever any stars put on a show, the class would be full up with new members. It would stay like that for a few weeks then the membership would drop off again, as the beginners found out just how hard they had to work.

"Oh good, Alex. I was hoping you'd be here tonight," said Liz, gliding up. "I wanted you to take the beginners for me, just for half an hour. I promised to go through the Inter-Silver dances with Diane and Nigel."

"Me?" said Alex who had never taught before. "You're sure? I mean, can they skate at all?"

"Most of them have been on the ice before. They can stand up — oh, you'll be all right. Just take them through a few basic steps." Then, before he could argue, she clapped her hands and raised her voice. "All beginners at the far end with Alex."

Alex watched as the beginners stumbled and struggled across the ice. Now he thought about it, he was going to enjoy this.

"All right, we'll have everybody in a line across the ice, to start with," he said. "I'll go in front and show you one or two steps and you can follow me." He took them to the barrier and they used that to help them turn around. "Let's have another try," said Alex. "Now look, you push off with the blade of the skate, not the spikes on the front." He took them to the middle again, getting them used to the feel of the ice. Alex wasn't feeling nearly as happy now, because the girl on the end was Samantha, and they were both pretending they hadn't seen one another.

Alex stuck to the very basic dance steps because, although most of them had skated before, none of them really knew what they were doing. After half an hour, six of them looked a bit better, going forward anyway. Three of them spent the whole time giggling, and he knew they wouldn't turn up for class again, and two more seemed to spend the whole time sitting on the ice. At last, Liz came skating over.

"Thanks, Alex, I'll take over now," she said. "Claire's looking for someone to go through the Bronze dances, if you could."

"What's happened to Jason?"

"Banged his knee and went to sit down," said Liz dryly.

"Aw, poor Jason," grinned Alex.

"Now, don't start, we can't all be tough hockey players," said Liz. "Anyway, it'll do you good. There's another Bronze test coming up in four months' time." Liz was pushing Alex to take his

Bronze again and he didn't want to, so he avoided answering by skating away. He did a flashy turn in front of the beginners and sat down with a thump on the hard surface. Everyone collapsed with laughter and he scrambled up and hurried off, his face bright red.

He found Claire and they partnered up and went around the ice a couple of times. Claire wasn't nearly as good as Alex but she was better than nobody.

"Diane said she had to dump you," said Claire. "She said you didn't even try at the test."

"Did she?" said Alex, not giving anything away.

"I'd hate it if Jason did that to me," said Claire. "Didn't you want to pass, or something?"

"No, I just wanted to throw money away," said Alex. "Now look, you've really got to cut a deeper edge on that curve. That's why you're drifting off."

"Who are you going to skate with for the next one?" asked Claire. Alex sighed and brought them to a halt in a shower of ice.

"Jason's gone off to have a break, has he?"

"Yes, he's hurt his knee."

"Oh, I thought it might be to give his ears a rest," said Alex. "Now shall we try it again? Because I'll tell you straight, you're a long way from Bronze standards."

The beginners' class was just finishing up, much to Alex's relief. It meant he could avoid meeting Samantha face to face. Liz took him aside.

"How did things go with the beginners?" she asked.

"OK, I suppose. A couple were all right."

"One of them says she's in your class at school."

"Yeah, Samantha Stephens — Miss Personality!"

"She seemed very good."

"Oh she's good all right. She's the best of that group by far," said Alex. "She's a liar, too! She told me the other night she'd never been on the ice before."

"She hasn't."

"Huh! No one skates like that first time."

"Alex, she's an ex-dancer, a very serious ex-dancer," said Liz. "Her balance is already perfect, and she'll know more about the structure of dance than anybody else here."

"Oh good," said Alex, "that makes me like her even more."

As Alex expected, most of the beginners soon dropped off, but Samantha stayed. He didn't have much to do with her. They didn't deliberately avoid each other but they were working on different things. At school, she still ignored him, but then again she ignored most people.

The Bronze test came and Alex managed to miss it by taking two weeks off. Liz was more upset than cross. The week he came back she partnered up with him, and they went through the three

Bronze Medal dances: the Fourteen Step, European Waltz, and the Foxtrot.

"You should've taken it, Alex. You'd have passed easily," she said seriously, as they paused to get their breath back.

"That's what you said last time," he said.

"I was right too, you shouldn't have failed!"

"If I'd have been skating with you, Liz, I'd have probably done better." said Alex.

"You could have. It was you that wanted a permanent partner," said Liz. "*I* didn't recommend Diane to you. I never thought you were suited for one minute."

"I know, it was me who pushed you," said Alex. "Between you and me I don't really like skating on my own. There doesn't seem much point."

"So in spite of all the tough act, you are really looking for someone else?" said Liz.

"Of course I am," said Alex. He gestured around the ice. "But there isn't anyone, is there?"

"Hm," Liz mused. "Why don't you ask the new girl?"

"Samantha? Don't be ridiculous. She can't stand the sight of me."

"Oh rubbish, she's just shy, that's all."

"Ha, that's what I thought — and it cost me a dollar," said Alex. "I'll pass, thank you."

"She's the only skater I've got at your level."

"Well, that makes me feel really good! I've been

skating on and off for four years. She's just started."

"It was a compliment, Alex — she's going to be good," said Liz. "I told you, it's her background in dance — she's going to be *very* good!"

"The next Bronze is, in what — four months? Are you seriously saying that she'll be ready to win it with me?"

"No, but she'll soon catch up," said Liz. She stood watching him as he thought about it. "You're the one looking for a partner, Alex."

"Yes, but one that could be a help to me, not a beginner."

"You know she passed her Novice last month?"

"What? She can't have been skating more than five months!"

"And she's asked me to put her in for next month's Preliminaries. She'll catch you up in no time."

"She's beginning to make me feel sick," said Alex. He shook his head. "It won't work, Liz, I don't want to end up with another Diane." He turned and skated off after the rest of the class. When he was gone, Samantha appeared from D exit where she had been hiding.

"What'd he say?" she said in a small voice.

"Oh, he'll come around," said Liz with a smile.

"You mean he said no?"

"No, he said maybe," said Liz. "He just needs a little nudge, that's all."

# 5.
# Partners?

Alex helped himself to a sandwich from the bag Toby was offering him. He took a huge bite, chewed it for a moment, and a look of horror spread across his face.

"What the heck is that?" he demanded.

"Shrimp, cream cheese, and pineapple," said Toby. "I'm trying out a new sandwich."

"Well, try it on somebody else, will you?" said Alex, handing it back in disgust. Toby took the top off his sandwich and regarded the filling worriedly.

"Hm, I don't think I've got it quite right yet," he said. "A bit more pepper, do you think?"

The two boys were sitting at the back of the class, waiting for Mr. J.B. Smith, the math teacher.

"And if you lose tomorrow night you're out of the whole tournament?" said Toby.

"Afraid so," said Alex. "We've already lost one and this team is really good."

"You shouldn't go in thinking you're going to lose," said Toby seriously.

"You haven't seen them!" said Alex. "They're all built like houses!" He emptied his books out on his desk and sighed. "I sure could do without a double dose of J.B."

"You've done the homework, I hope?"

"Not really," said Alex.

"What do you mean — not really?" demanded Toby.

"It means *no*! All right? I didn't have time last night. We had a special hockey practice before dance class."

"That's it — you're dead!" said Toby. "I only hope — " Toby broke off at the sound of heavy footsteps. "Take cover, here comes J.B.!"

Mr. J.B. Smith didn't waste time saying hello. The first thing he said concerned mathematics and it was an instruction to Jean Taylor to collect the homework. When she reached Alex's desk, he shook his head. "Cover for me, Jeannie," he whispered.

"What? I can't! He'll notice," she said.

"Oh, go on, I'll add it to the pile later. He'll leave them on the shelf outside the staff room."

"Thanks," she said, grimacing and going off in a huff.

"That's not fair," Toby said quietly. "She's the one who'll get into trouble."

"Aw, he won't notice," Alex said uneasily.

"This is J.B. Smith we're talking about!"

"Yes! Yes! Yes!" said Alex testily. He sighed and raised his hand. "Sir."

"What is it, Barnes?" demanded Mr. J.B. Smith.

"I don't seem to have my homework book with me," said Alex.

"How sad." Mr. J.B. Smith didn't look sad.

"You see sir, I had to . . ."

"Barnes, I don't want to know," Mr. J.B. Smith interrupted. "You know the rules: one hour's detention tomorrow night."

"But I can't, sir, I'm playing in an ice hockey match!"

"Can't?" Mr. J.B. Smith gave Alex one of his "looks." "Oh, I think you can, Barnes!" He turned back to the blackboard. Alex glared at Toby.

"You and your mouth," he said.

"How is this my fault?" said Toby. "I wanted to watch the hockey match as much as you wanted to play it — more, knowing you."

"Well, nothing's stopping you from going, is there?" Alex raised his hand again.

"Sir?"

"What is it now, Barnes?" Mr. J.B. Smith said wearily.

"Couldn't I stay for detention tonight, sir? I really am needed on the hockey team."

Mr. J.B. Smith sighed. "You know what the Headmaster says, Barnes, detention is always the following evening so you have time to warn your parents about being late home. You're in detention tomorrow night, Barnes, and that's all there is to it."

"Mr. Smith, sir," a voice said. He turned to find the new girl, Samantha Stephens, with her hand in the air. Mr. J.B. Smith was surprised. He couldn't remember her ever speaking in class before.

"Yes, er — Samantha?" he said more gently.

"It's not Alex's fault about his book," she said. "It's mine. We're in the same skating class and I borrowed it last night. I must have left it at home."

"He lent it to you?"

"Yes, sir. You remember, you told me to copy the work I was behind on." She gazed at him with serious eyes.

"Oh — er, yes," said Mr. J.B. Smith. "All right then, Barnes, you're off the hook! Make sure I get it tomorrow, will you?"

"Yes, sir, thank you, sir," said Alex. When Mr. J.B. Smith's back was turned Alex found Toby's eyes boring into him.

"Was that true?" Toby demanded.

"You heard what she said, didn't you?" said Alex, and he started taking an unusual interest in quadratic equations.

They were skating in pairs on Wednesday night. Liz partnered up with Samantha trying to show her how to cut her edges deeper. Samantha could already dance better than anybody else in the class but her skating often let her down.

"Now here," said Liz as they raced towards the edge of the ice, "change from one edge to the other. That's the way — no turn, faster! Watch out for the barriers!" She stopped them dead and had to hang on to Samantha to keep her from going over.

"Sorry," gasped Samantha. "We were always taught to use the whole floor."

"Yes, that's right, it's the same with ice skating," said Liz. "But you have to bear in mind you're traveling much faster — and it's more difficult to stop."

"Do you lose many points if you fall?"

"You lose points, yes, but it's more you ruin the whole effect." She regarded the girl for a moment, "You said anything to Alex yet?"

"No."

"Well, I would. He is the best choice for you," said Liz. "He's quite talented and your arms are the same length. That's important. It makes the whole thing look better. I'll have another word with him."

"Oh no, please," said Samantha hurriedly, "I'd rather the suggestion came from him."

"Oh, I see." Liz sighed. "Look Samantha, does it really matter?"

"It's not what you think."

"No?"

"No! I do have a very good reason for wanting him to ask me. It's just that I don't really want to tell anybody about it."

"Well, I'd get it sorted out soon if I were you or one of the others will snap him up — there's always more girls than boys in skating."

Samantha showered as quickly as she could. They were running late because of the hockey match and she had to get home. She changed and put her skates in the locker she had rented. None of the others had lockers, they were really for the coaches, but Samantha had to keep her skating a secret from her parents. If they found out, that would be the end of it. Ice skating had filled the void left by the loss of dancing, and it had filled it more than she had ever dreamed.

She brushed her hair in the mirror and put on some lipstick so her parents would think she'd been out with friends. The clock said it was nearly ten and she swore under her breath. It would be dark by the time she got home and her dad would start moaning again. She dashed down the stairs and out into the car park, then she stopped dead.

Alex was sitting on the car-park wall, giving her a wry grin.

"You sure take your time getting changed," he said.

"I didn't realize it was a race."

He slid off the wall. "I was going in that direction." He pointed. "Any objection to me walking beside you?"

"It's a free country," said Samantha, knowing he was lying. She had found out where he lived weeks before. They walked in silence. Surprisingly, it was Samantha who broke it.

"Did you win your hockey match?"

"Yeah, we did," said Alex. "Best game we've ever played. Toby nearly burst a blood vessel."

"What? Playing?"

"No, not Toby — cheering," said Alex. "Look, are you going to tell me why you stuck your neck out for me in math?"

"I was the only one with a reason to borrow your book," Samantha said. "He was bound to believe me."

"You could've ended up in detention yourself, knowing J.B."

"I wasn't doing anything special. I could be late for dance class one time."

"Thanks anyway," he said. "It still doesn't tell me why you did it."

She shrugged. "At my old school we always helped each other out, especially when it affected training."

There was another embarrassed silence. This time it was Alex who broke it.

"Liz suggests we try being partners," he said. Then he went on in a rush: "Just on a trial basis, you understand?"

"Does she?"

"Yes. She says you'd rather dance with a partner."

"I suppose I'm more used to it."

"Well, what d'you think?"

"I'm not sure. I haven't really thought about it," she said. "I suppose it wouldn't hurt to give it a try, but I think you should be careful."

"Why?"

"Because I might have to give up skating very suddenly," she said.

"Like you did dancing, you mean?"

"Just like I did dancing!"

"Why?"

She gave another shrug. "Oh, reasons," she said evasively. "Think of it: months and months of work, then bang, one night — all over!"

"That's an ice skater's life," said Alex. "One fall and that's it."

"Well, I've warned you," she said. "I still think I'm a bad risk."

"I'll chance it," said Alex.

"OK then," she said. "Now don't you think you'd better turn around? Or you're never going to get home tonight."

# 6.
# More Than Just
# a Hobby

On Monday Alex and Samantha skated together for the first time. The minute Alex took his new partner in his arms he knew he had found something special. Diane had felt like a sack of coal compared to Samantha, whose suppleness and strength were amazing. She looked so right, and the way she moved to the music was so assured, so relaxed.

He stopped after one circuit of the ice.

"Are you seriously telling me you've only been skating for six months?" he demanded.

"Five months today," she said. "Can't you tell?"

"No, I cannot! I'd have said you'd been skating for years," he said. "Your dancing moves are just about perfect — certainly better than mine. Even the way you hold your hands!"

She gave a small smile. "Pity my skating's not as good, isn't it?"

"That'll come."

"Not standing here talking, it won't!" She took

his hand and started them off again. Alex always treated dance class as a bit of fun after the rigors of hockey, but Samantha skated like she was out to win. She never stopped for a breather and never seemed to want one, but Alex did, he was rapidly running out of energy. He looked for an escape, but Liz was leaving them alone to get used to one another.

"Hold on a sec," he gasped, coming to a halt.

"What's up?" said Samantha.

"Aaaah." Alex drew in a huge breath. "Er — nothing, I just thought we could . . ." He broke off and looked around to make sure Liz wasn't watching, ". . . um, perhaps we could try a lift?"

"Fine by me — let's do it. We don't want to get cold."

"No, of course not," said Alex.

"Have you done many lifts?"

"A few low ones with Diane. They didn't go that well," he admitted.

"Well, as long as you're strong enough to support me."

"Sure, you must weigh half of what Diane does."

"I wouldn't let her hear you say that," said Samantha dryly.

So when Liz turned to see how the two new partners were getting along, she found Alex skating along with Samantha held high. Liz grabbed for her whistle, then paused. That was as likely to make them fall as anything. She hurried across

42

the ice. Alex saw her coming and eased Samantha back down again.

"What are you doing, Alex?" Liz demanded.

"Oh, I knew I'd get the blame," he said.

"You're supposed to know what you're doing!"

"We were just trying a few lifts, Liz," said Samantha.

"This is your first night together, for heaven's sake!" said Liz. "Anyway, we don't use high lifts in ice dancing."

"I'm used to lifts," said Samantha.

"Not on ice you're not!"

"Believe me, I've hit the floor lots of times."

"Ice is not a sprung floor," said Liz. "Now, do as I say please — both of you!"

"Wow, she's pretty mad at us," said Alex when Liz had skated away.

"That's mad?" said Samantha.

"As bad as it gets."

Samantha smiled, "I really must introduce you to a ballet teacher I once had."

"Anyway, we were quite safe, weren't we?" said Alex.

"Not really," said Samantha. "You're not strong enough yet."

"Hey, now look here . . ."

"It wasn't an insult," said Samantha. "The boys at dance school used to do a hundred push-ups every morning."

"I can do that!" said Alex crossly.

"Hm," said Samantha, not sounding convinced. "I think your skating's great though. I can hardly keep up with you."

"That's the hockey," said Alex, pacified. "You'll be OK when we dance to music. We have to keep to the tempo then — oh, you know that of course." He looked at her to see if she was laughing at him but she wasn't. "I suppose we'd better go through the waltz, tango, and foxtrot if you're serious about taking the Preliminaries next month."

"Of course I'm serious," she said.

"Who are you taking them with?"

"You," she said bluntly.

"Eh? You're joking?"

"Why? Don't you want to be my partner?" she said. "I thought it seemed to be working quite well."

"Yes, of course, but I naturally assumed you'd skate the test with one of the male coaches — or Simon. He's got his inter-Silver."

"No way! You're my partner."

"Yes." He paused. "Look, Sam . . ."

She made a face. "Do you mind? I hate being called Sam."

"Oh — right. Look, Samantha, usually you skate your medal test with someone a lot better than you are — it helps."

"You are better than me," she said.

"I only hope I don't mess it up for you," he said worriedly.

"Don't you think it would be a good idea to have an extra night's practice each week? Other than dance class, I mean."

"I suppose so," said Alex. "It's just that I'm here Friday nights as well, for the hockey matches."

"How about Thursday then? We can have a good long session together."

"You're sure you can manage three nights a week?"

"I think it'll be all right," she said. "Anyway, I think we've got to — the Bronze medal tests are only four months away you know."

"Yes — so Liz was saying," he said. Then he froze. "You're not seriously thinking of taking those as well, are you?"

"Yes."

"But . . . but, you can't!" he protested. "The Bronze test's no picnic, you know."

"Yeah, so I've heard," she said. Then she added casually, "When I won my Silver medal for dance, only two of us passed out of seven." She stood gazing at him levelly.

"Oh," he said. "But . . . *I* wasn't planning on taking the Bronze over again so soon."

"Look, I'll explain it to you," she said. "I was trying to be a professional dancer. I can't even remember a time when I wasn't going to be a dancer — and now that's all gone! If ice dancing is going to replace that it means doing it well, and that means taking the medals, doesn't it?"

"Well, yes," he said. "Look, Sam . . . Samantha . . ."

"Alex, I've come into skating late as it is, so I haven't time to mess around," she said. "If we're going to be partners you've a right to know that this is more than a hobby for me."

"There's a lot more things in life than ice skating."

"No, there's not! There's nothing in life *but* ice skating, not if we're going to get anywhere." She held out her arms to him. "C'mon, you must have gotten your breath back by now."

Alex deliberately hung back at the end of the class so he could speak to Liz. When everybody else had gone, he skated across to where she was sorting out the music cassettes.

She looked over her shoulder at him and grinned. "She's got you worried then?" she said.

"How do you know?" he demanded.

"By your hair." She patted his hair back in place. He stepped back out of her reach.

"She's a bit serious, Liz."

"I thought that might be a problem."

"She's crazy! She's not thinking of Preliminaries and ordinary stuff like that. She's planning her next career move after she's got the Olympic Gold!"

"Sounds a healthy attitude to me."

"But Liz, she wants us to win the next Bronze — both of us!"

"Does she?" Liz thought for a moment. "It's possible I suppose, but it means a lot of work."

"Oh she's figured that out already," he said. "She's got me skating on a Thursday as well. That's four nights for me and three for her!"

"She's been doing five nights since she started," said Liz.

"Geez, she never mentioned that," said Alex. "Tell me, is Diane still free?"

Liz smiled, "She's just what you need, Alex. I know she's a bit serious, but if someone doesn't push you along then you're never going to get anywhere."

"I didn't know that I was planning on getting anywhere!"

"That would be a great pity," said Liz. "Look, if she didn't think you were the best male skater in the club she wouldn't have chosen you for a partner."

"Chosen me? I chose her!" he said indignantly.

"Oh yes, I forgot." Liz picked up the music system and carried it up the stairs. Alex couldn't figure out why she was laughing.

*　　*　　*

47

Samantha ran up the hill. She had been running for over two miles now but was hardly out of breath. Her father's car was in the driveway and at the sight of it she swore softly. Her parents had been to a meeting at the school and Samantha had been hoping to beat them home.

They were waiting for her in the living room.

"Is that you, Samantha?" her mother's voice called.

"No, it's Tina Turner," Samantha muttered, then out loud, "Yes, Mommy," She stuck her head round the door. "I'm just going upstairs. I've got a ton of homework to do."

"You come in here, young lady," said her father severely. "We want a word with you." Samantha crept into the room and perched herself on the very edge of the couch.

"I really do have a lot of homework, Daddy," she said. "Can't it wait until tomorrow?"

"No, it can't!" said her father sharply. "We've just seen your report card."

"Oh," she said in a small voice. "I've only just started to settle in."

"Evidently!"

"I'm trying to catch up."

"Your Headmaster says you're not even trying," said her father. "He says you don't even make an effort to fit in with the rest of your class."

"Well, they're all so childish! All they worry about is what's on the charts or on TV."

48

"But they still do better than you at school, don't they?" said her father.

"And if you don't have any school friends, who are you meeting when you go out every night?" asked her mother.

"I do have some friends."

"Your teacher says you don't," said her father.

"How would she know? She doesn't even speak to me."

"Perhaps if you stayed in a bit more you'd have more time for your schoolwork."

"If I don't go walking, I can't sleep," said Samantha. "My body's used to exercise. Even the doctor told you that."

"Yes, well, that may be," said her father, "but we've got to do something. What are you planning on doing when you leave school without any qualifications?"

"You know what I wanted to do," blurted out Samantha, "and you took that away from me!"

"That's not fair, Samantha," said her mother, angry for the first time. Mr. Stephens looked hurt but he didn't say anything.

"If we stopped you from dancing it was for your own good," was all he said.

"My own good?" Samantha demanded. "You just don't know what you did!"

"Now darling, no one's blaming you," said her mother more reasonably. "We know you've been through a difficult time. It's partly our fault, taking you away from Tracy Powell's and sending you to a day school in mid-term, but we wanted you near us — we nearly lost you, you know?"

"Yes, I think we made a wrong decision," said Mr. Stephens.

"You mean you're thinking of sending me back to dance school?" said Samantha, wide-eyed.

"No! No! No!" said her father hurriedly.

"Darling, you know there isn't a dance school in the country that would take you," said her mother. "No, your father's been making inquiries about a very nice boarding school in Sussex."

"What?" Samantha demanded, coming to her feet.

"It's in a beautiful spot, and there's a theater where the girls put on school plays. You could . . ."

"No!" Samantha shouted. "I won't go! I won't! If you try and make me I'll run away! I swear it! I swear it!" Samantha ran out of the room and they heard her pounding up the stairs.

"That went well," sighed her father.

"She's at a difficult age, Donald."

"She's been at a difficult age since the day she was born," said Mr. Stephens. "It appears she likes this new school better than we thought."

"Hm — I wonder," said Mrs. Stephens.

Samantha lay on her bed staring at the ceiling. On the wall facing her was a poster of Mikhail

Baryshnikov and another one of Natalia Maka-rova, the two ballet dancers. The posters were old and faded, as they had followed Samantha everywhere for years. Recently a new one had appeared, but it was stuck behind the doorway so it wasn't so noticeable.

The door opened and her mother came in. She sat down on the side of the bed and Samantha leaned forward and put her arms around her.

"I didn't mean to hurt Daddy's feelings," she said after a minute.

"You never do, do you?" said her mother. "We just want what's best for you, darling."

"Don't send me away, then."

"Do you think we want to? We just thought you might be more settled at another boarding school."

"I don't want to change schools again," said Samantha. "If I can't go back to Tracy Powell's I'd rather stay where I am. I certainly don't want to go to a school where a bunch of idiot girls put on school plays!"

"Samantha, just because people don't dance, doesn't necessarily mean they're idiots," her mother sighed. Samantha didn't answer.

"All right then, Samantha," her mother said, "we'll leave it until the end of next term, but if your grades haven't improved by then we've got to do something."

"They will have."

"So, are you going to tell me about these walks of yours?"

"I just go for walks, that's all — there's nothing wrong in that."

"And you meet friends, do you?"

"Some — they're all right, Mommy, honest."

"I think I can trust you not to be silly," said Mrs. Stephens. "And how about this boy you're meeting? What's he like?"

"Who told you about him?" Samantha demanded.

"You just did," said her mother. Samantha bit her lip and avoided her mother's eyes.

"Come on now, darling, I'm not stupid, you know."

"There is a boy," said Samantha at last. "He's not a boyfriend. He's — well, you know. Just someone to talk to."

"Is he nice?

"Hm."

"And how old is he?"

"The same as me, I think. He's in my class at school," said Samantha. Then, suddenly realizing there was something she could say without lying, she added, "I go and watch him play hockey — and others are there from the school, too."

"Why didn't you tell us?" said her mother. "Surely you didn't have to make a big secret out of it?"

"Daddy still thinks I'm a little girl," said Samantha.

"Well, you shouldn't act like one, should you?" said her mother, standing up. She went to the door, "Hm, that's new," she said noticing the poster for the first time. "Who are they?"

"Er, Torvill and Dean, one of the girls at school gave it to me," said Samantha.

"Thought I recognized them," said Mrs. Stephens. "You'd better bring this boy home one evening, so we can meet him. What did you say his name was?"

"I didn't, but it's Alex," said Samantha.

"All right, then. Don't forget your homework."

Samantha sat gazing at her posters, listening to her mother's footsteps fading down the stairs.

"Oh, terrific," she said savagely.

# 7.
# Pride and a Fall

Hello, what are those?" Alex asked as Samantha came warily down the steps. She was wearing a gleaming brand-new pair of skates.

"I ordered them a few weeks ago," she said. "To celebrate passing my Preliminary."

"You didn't know you were going to pass until Saturday," he said, kneeling down to examine them.

"Well, if I'd failed they would've cheered me up," she said.

He looked up. "Samantha, these are Belati Golds!"

"What's wrong with that? Aren't they any good?"

"They're just about the best skates made," he said. "You must have more money than sense — I think Diane's the only other person in the club with proper dance skates."

"Aren't yours dance skates then?"

"No they're not! They're recreational dance skates."

"What does that mean?"

"It means I'm poor!"

"So am I, now. I had some of my tuition fees left from Tracey Powell's and my dad told me to invest the money — so I did," she said. She had been gazing with pride at her new skates and when she looked up, Alex had an angry look on his face. She went up to him. "Seriously, Alex, what are recreational skates?"

"They're the ones you buy with blades already fitted," he snapped.

"What are you getting so uptight about?" demanded Samantha.

"Can you blame me? Four years I've been skating! Four bloody years, and I've just managed to persuade my mom to buy me a pair of skates — that's the second pair you've had this year," he said.

"Oh, c'mon, don't be such a pain!" she said. "I want to try them out."

They went around the ice a few times getting warmed up. Samantha kept putting in extra flashy steps to see how her skates felt. When it came down to it she couldn't really see much difference between the new skates and her old cheap pair, but she knew she needed to get used to them. The rest of the class were congregating at the far end of the rink, so they skated over to join them. Liz hadn't arrived yet.

"Hey, well done on your Prelim, Sam," said Barry.

"I simply don't know what took you so long," said Melanie. "I mean, just because the rest of us had been skating years before we dared take a Medal Test."

"Ah, but you don't have our Sam's talent, do you?" grinned Steve. Samantha gave her small smile at the others' banter. She got along much better with the skaters than with the pupils at school.

"Quite the little star, aren't we?" said a cold voice. Samantha turned. Diane had the usual sneer on her face.

"Oh, no, Diane, you're the star," said Samantha managing to make it sound rude. "We *all* know that — and if we don't, your mother lets us know."

"I'm surprised you've got anywhere dragging him around with you!" Diane said, jerking her thumb in Alex's direction.

"Boring!" said Alex. To his surprise, Samantha linked her arm through his.

"Alex is the main reason I passed," she said very clearly. "He helped me every step of the way — you wouldn't understand about that, would you, Diane?"

"Don't get too big for your skates just because

you struggled your way through the Prelims," sneered Diane. "And make sure you stay out of my way, will you? I can't stand beginners cluttering up the ice."

"Oh, go suck a lemon, Diane," sighed Alex. "Liz is here now."

"You might be scared of Liz, but I'm not," said Diane. "My mother practically employs her!"

"Pity she doesn't employ the judges, isn't it?" said Samantha. "Or perhaps she does?" Alex took Samantha's hand and virtually dragged her away across the ice from what looked like turning into a physical fight.

"She's not worth arguing with," he said.

"Ha! Everyone's worth arguing with," said Samantha.

"Was that true what you said back there? About me helping you?"

"Course it was," said Samantha. "Oh, the dances were easy enough but I needed you to give me confidence. Anyway, you helped me keep my momentum up."

"I'm glad I'm still useful for something," he said. "Now, what have you got planned for tonight? I suppose it's too much to hope you'll let us take it easy after Saturday's success?"

"We're going to go over the Bronze dances, of course," she said, surprised.

"I shouldn't have bothered to ask," he said. "C'mon, I'll take you through them."

Halfway through the session Sue skated over. She bent down and admired Samantha's skates. Then, when she stood up again, she asked:

"Can I borrow Alex for five minutes, Sam?"

"Sure, but I want him back in good shape mind, he's still under guarantee," said Samantha. Alex paired up with Sue and she started them off around the ice, just doing simple steps and three turns.

"What d'you want me for?" he demanded.

"I needed a partner to practice with for a bit, that's all."

"Just like all solo skaters, do you mean?" he said. "Sure, I've known you too long, what do you really want?"

She smiled. "OK, it's about Diane."

"Oh, her! What's up *now?*"

"Well, I rather think she's out to get you."

"Oh, well done, Sherlock! So what else is new?"

"I'm serious, Alex," she said earnestly. "Someone's put it around what really happened at your Bronze test and suddenly everybody's on your side."

"Yeah?" said Alex, pleased. "I wonder who did that — eh, Sue?"

She shrugged, "It wasn't me, actually, though I do know who it was," she said. "You'll have to keep it to yourself."

"Of course."

"It was Liz."

"Liz?"

"Yes, she must've gotten fed up with everything Diane's been saying about you," said Samantha. "And now Nigel's going, everybody's taken to calling her 'Desperate Diane' — get it? Desperate for a partner?"

"What's happening to Nigel?"

"I thought you'd have heard," said Sue. "His parents are moving to America in about six months."

"America? That's bad luck for her," said Alex.

"Yes, and, knowing Diane, she's got to take it out on somebody," said Sue. "I'm warning you, Alex, watch out for her. She's a nasty piece of work."

Alex and Samantha had progressed to low lifts and they stayed behind after class to practice them. Samantha had him working on a lateral lift where he had to hold her horizontal to the ice. He couldn't quite manage it without wobbling, but she didn't panic like the other girls he skated with, just stayed there precariously in the air waiting for him to get it right.

"No," said Samantha, as Alex hurriedly dumped her back on the ice. "You're far too tense — relax a bit."

"You told me to lock my arms — you said I wasn't strong enough," he protested.

"That's right, but it doesn't mean you have to tense your whole body," she said. "How are the push-ups coming on?"

"What push-ups?"

"Oh, you've not managed the hundred yet, then?" she said wickedly.

"Well, how many can you do?"

"I've never tried to do more than a hundred at a time," she said airily.

"Ha!" he said, using one of her expressions without realizing it.

"Let's try again," she said. "And this time keep your body more relaxed."

"How can I relax? I might drop you!"

"So drop me, I'm not made of glass," she said.

"I might damage your skates," he said sarcastically. She stood and regarded him, her hands on her hips.

"If they're going to bother you that much, I'll wear the other ones in future," she said.

"It was just a joke."

"Yeah, it sounded like one," she said wearily. "Can we get on with it, Alex? we're wasting time."

They skated around the ice to pick up momentum then Alex lifted her up again, wobbled a bit, managed to correct it, then there was a tremendous thump as someone crashed into them. Alex managed to catch himself but Samantha was flung onto the ice with a crash.

"So sorry," called Diane, skating away.

"You silly cow!" Alex yelled after her. He rushed over to Samantha but she was already picking herself up. "You all right, Sam?"

"Of course," she said crossly, "and it's Samantha — remember?"

"Sorry, I'm sure," he said. "Positive you're not hurt?"

"I've told you, Alex, I've been there before. Now let's try it again, shall we?"

Alex was used to getting changed fast but, that night, Samantha beat him to it. She was waiting for him outside.

"What are you doing here?" he asked.

"Waiting for you."

"Oh — what for?"

"I wanted to ask a favor," she said. "I wondered whether you'd mind walking me home?"

"What?" he demanded. "Why the change of heart all of a sudden? You're not afraid of the dark, are you?"

"No."

"Oh, I get it, you think Diane might be lying in wait?" he joked.

"I only wish she was," said Samantha fervently. "No, it's just — well, my parents want to meet you. They're making a bit of a fuss about me being out late at night."

"If you'd agreed to that early on it would've saved me a dollar," said Alex. "Of course I'll walk you home. I only hope they won't interrogate me."

"Don't worry, they won't!" she said, then smiled. "Well, not much anyway."

They walked down the road, their conversation stilted now they were outside the rink. At last, they turned off up a side road, and Samantha gave a sigh, knowing what was going to happen.

"You live up here?" said Alex, eyeing the big houses.

"Yes."

"Geez, what does your dad do?"

"He's an accountant," she said. Suddenly she stopped and turned him to face her. "Look, Alex, I'm not going to apologize because my dad's well-off," she said. "He's only being generous with money at the moment because he took me out of dance school."

"Makes no difference to me what your dad does for a living!" Alex said.

"The heck it doesn't! You've been a real pain all night long!"

"Well, it's so easy for you! You have no idea the problems I have to keep on skating," he said. "I can't afford skates, I can't afford the entrance money — clothes, anything! If I didn't have my paper route I wouldn't even be able to keep my head above water — all you have to do is ask!"

"We all have problems, Alex," she said in a small voice.

"Oh sure. What problems do you have?"

"Well, I've got a big one coming up in about a minute," she said.

"What?"

"You're about to meet my parents," she said.

"And that's a problem?" he demanded. "What's the matter, Sam? Aren't I good enough for them?"

"Oh don't be such a jerk!"

"Well, what?"

"My parents don't know I skate."

"They what?"

"They don't know I skate. And they mustn't!" she said. "They just think we all meet in the arcade and I watch you play hockey — I haven't even said it's ice hockey."

"But . . . ?" He broke off. "Why, for heaven's sake?"

"Because if they find out they'll stop me," she said. "They won't let me do any exercise, you see."

"Won't let you do any exercise?" he demanded. "Why on earth not?"

"Oh, it's a lot of nonsense!" she said. "They still think I'm delicate!"

"Delicate?" he repeated in an awed voice. "You're about as delicate as Mike Tyson!"

"Yes, well," she said. "Just humor them for me, will you?"

"But Samantha, you can't keep something like that a secret."

"I don't see why not," she said. "I always leave

63

my skates at the rink. There's no reason why they should find out anything, if you watch your mouth."

He was still staring blankly at her and now his hair was all messed up again. "So you want me to . . . ?"

"Lie to them, yes," said Samantha bluntly.

"Well, what about these?" He held up his skate bag.

"Leave them in the bushes at the end of the driveway," said Samantha, who had already thought this out.

Alex's expression slowly relaxed into a grin. "OK," he said. "I can handle it."

They started walking down the road again. Neither of them spoke for a full minute, then Samantha gazed up at him.

"We're friends again now?" she said.

He laughed. "Yes, Samantha, sorry," he said. "I won't moan about being broke anymore — at least my life's simple."

# 8.
# Play It Again, Sam

I thought they were very nice to me, considering," said Alex to Samantha. They were standing in a line of skaters as they repeated the same sequence of steps, again and again.

"What did you expect them to do? Eat you?" said Samantha.

"Yeah, well it's just that I don't really like lying to them."

"You think I do?" she demanded, stopping dead to stare at him.

Liz blew her whistle. "Do you mind, *Sam?*"

"Sorry," she muttered and got back to her position. She waited a minute until Liz's eyes were off her. "Look Alex, I don't like lying to them but it's either that or stop skating altogether — I've got no other choice."

Liz blew her whistle again and Samantha automatically said sorry before she realized it wasn't aimed at her.

"Gather around everybody," Liz said. "Now,

it's only three months to the Maria Aitkiss competition and I need some names. Remember, this is really for those of you working for the inter-Silver, that sort of standard."

Alex looked around. There were seven couples with their hands up, Diane and Nigel among them. He was never going to like Diane but he felt sorry for the way she was building herself up for this competition only to have her partnership break up soon afterwards.

"See there's some advantage in failing your Bronze," he said turning to Samantha. He gulped. She had her hand in the air.

"Put your hand down, you idiot," he said.

"Ha! You put yours up!"

"But . . ."

"Put your hand up!" She gave him a shove. "C'mon, don't be such a wimp!" Reluctantly, he slid his hand half in the air. When Liz finished with the others and turned to them he pretended he was scratching his head.

Liz came over. "I think it might be a bit soon for you two," she said, in a friendly tone.

"We'll be all right," said Samantha. She gestured to Alex with her thumb. "Mr. Enthusiasm here had his hand up but he got tired."

"The qualification for entering is that you must have your Bronze medal," said Liz. "Like I said, it's really aimed at those working for inter-Silver and above."

"When is it?" Samantha asked.

"In three months — on the twenty-eighth."

"Fine, that's a month after the Bronze test," said Samantha. "If we pass we'll be working for our inter-Silver by then, won't we? Put our names down."

Liz sighed. "Sam, the Maria Aitkiss competition comprises two compulsory dances from the junior tests, which you should be fine on, but then there's a three-minute free dance! You haven't even thought about a free dance yet, and we simply don't have the time to put one together."

"We'll manage, Liz," said Samantha. "It'll be good experience anyway, won't it, Alex?"

"It won't," said Alex. "There's no way I'm going to enter."

"Oh, he will, Liz," said Samantha.

"Don't bet on it!" said Alex crossly. He grabbed Samantha's hand and dragged her off across the ice, skating so furiously that she could hardly keep up with him.

"Hey, slow down a bit," she gasped after their fifth furious circuit. He stopped dead and glared at her.

"You made us look like a couple of jerks!" he said crossly. "It's bad enough in front of Liz, but in front of all the others? In front of Diane!"

"Don't worry about it, Alex," she said calmly. "Put your name down. We'll cope, no trouble."

"Samantha, there's a three-minute free dance!"

he said. "It takes months to put a free together, and years to get it right."

"Alex, don't fuss. I've been working on a free dance for us for weeks," said Samantha. "What d'you think all those lateral lifts are for?"

"You've what?" he demanded. Then he added, more reasonably: "Can you do that?"

"What do you imagine I've been doing for the last ten years?" she said. "I'll soon choreograph a three-minute dance for us. That's the least of our problems."

"Right now, I can't think of a bigger problem than that," he said.

"I can," she said. "When do we practice it?"

"We skate three nights together, isn't that enough?"

"We need the two dance classes to practice for the Bronze. Without that, it's all out the window anyway. That only leaves us Thursdays."

"Samantha, I can't skate any more nights," he said. "I'm already doing the two dance classes, Mondays and Wednesdays, then there's the session with you on a Thursday, and don't forget there's a hockey match every Friday night. My parents wouldn't let me anyway. We've had enough arguments about it already — I'm already behind with my homework as it is!"

She sighed, "Perhaps we could do some static work on it in the school gym — lunchtimes."

"You're kidding!" he said. "Samantha, I'll tell

you straight, you'll never get me to make a fool of myself at school! I can guess what the rest of the class would say."

"Does that worry you?" She seemed surprised.

"Yes, it does! And I'm not ashamed of it. Imagine the audience we'd get. The whole school would turn up to watch."

"All right, but Diane and Nigel are here most nights working on their free dance with that crazy woman — it's going to be hard to beat them."

"Beat them? Look, if we tried really hard, I mean *really* hard, we might come in a good last."

"Oh, Alex, don't be so negative," she said. "Who was Maria Aitkiss anyway?"

"Not was — is," he said. "You know that crazy woman you were talking about?"

"The one who looks like she has her hair done every day?"

"Yes. That's Maria Aitkiss," said Alex. "She's Diane's mother, if you must know. She was a Silver Medallist in the Europeans about a hundred years ago. I think she started this competition to remind everybody."

Samantha smiled. "I bet there's a massive cup for the winner."

"Heck yes, the biggest darn cup you ever saw," he said. "It's bigger than the one for the British Championships."

She stood gazing at him for a minute. "C'mon Alex, let's give it a try."

"I don't know, Samantha, seriously I don't," he said. "It's not as easy as that. I haven't even seen this free dance yet."

"Well, I can't show it to you just yet, it's not finished," she said.

"There you are then," he said. "I think we should just concentrate on the Bronze, see what happens."

She gave a resigned smile. "Oh, Alex, I do wish you'd believe in yourself more." She held out her arms to him, and they started off around the ice.

Dance class was no longer relaxation for Alex. Ever since that first night when he had paired up with Samantha it had become tougher than any hockey match. And longer. When he finally managed to get her to quit, the others had long gone, except for Liz.

"No, she hasn't talked me into it," said Alex.

"He wants time to think about it," said Samantha. "He thinks he's Winston Churchill."

"Um — I'm sorry Samantha, but the decision's been taken away from you," said Liz, looking embarrassed.

"What do you mean?" demanded Samantha.

"Mrs. Aitkiss has just been on the phone," said Liz. "She says that only people who already have their Bronze medals can put their names down."

"But we will have," protested Samantha.

"She says the closing date for entry is next weekend," said Liz.

"Closing date?" put in Alex. "I never heard of a closing date before."

"Mrs. Aitkiss says that hundreds of people come to watch her competition and she wants to keep the standards up," said Liz.

"Keep the standards up?" said Samantha loudly. "With her useless daughter entering? Who does she think she is? You aren't going to stand for this, are you, Liz? Surely you can . . . ?"

"Leave it, Samantha," said Alex. "It's not Liz's fault."

"She's the dance teacher, isn't she?"

"Yes — and she doesn't get paid for it," said Alex. Samantha subsided, biting her bottom lip. After a minute she said, "Yeah, I know. Sorry, Liz, I shouldn't have taken it out on you."

"The way I see it, the important thing is to keep the dance class going," said Liz. "Even if it isn't always fair."

"It's OK, Liz," said Alex. "We weren't going to enter anyway." He turned to Samantha, "C'mon, we'd better go home."

"Yeah," said Samantha. Then to Liz, "Just one last thing. I take it Diane called her mother earlier about this?"

Alex always stayed in bed on a Sunday morning. He lay there and stretched his feet luxuriously.

It was ten thirty and he knew that if he was there a bit longer, his mother would bring his breakfast up.

The door opened and his mother put her head around the door.

"Thanks, mom," said Alex sitting up, but his mother was empty-handed.

"There's a girl waiting downstairs for you," she said.

"Yeah?" said Alex. "Who?"

"I don't know her name," said Mrs. Barnes. "I've never seen her before."

"Jennie," said Alex positively. "I've not seen her for weeks." He suddenly froze. "Hang on, what's she like? A cross between Margaret Thatcher and a Rottweiler?"

"She seems quite sweet," said his mother. "I would hurry up if I were you — she'll be in the living room." She closed the door on him.

"Sweet," said Alex to himself. "I didn't know they still made girls who were sweet."

It was ten minutes before he was dressed, and he came hurrying into the living room to find Samantha sitting on the carpet doing a stretching exercise. She was dressed in a gray sweatsuit and sneakers.

"Boy, you sure do get up at the crack of dawn," she said.

"But my mother said it wasn't you," protested Alex.

"She doesn't even know who I am."

"I can assure you that the description she gave didn't quite fit," said Alex. "Anyway, it's not going to do you any good at all. There's no way you're going to talk me into entering this competition. I've been thinking about it; we were crazy to consider it. Even if Diane's mother hadn't put her foot in it, I still wouldn't enter."

"It's nothing to do with the competition," she said getting to her feet. "I thought you'd like to come for a run, that's all."

"What? A run! Why?" said Alex horrified.

"Because it's Sunday and the rink's closed," said Samantha. "I thought you might feel like a bit of exercise."

"But I haven't even had breakfast yet," he said plaintively.

"All the better, help you work up an appetite," she said. "Go and get some sneakers on."

"Aw, no, Samantha, running's not my idea of a good time," he protested. "If I have to go further than the end of the road I usually take a bus."

Half an hour later Alex was perspiring, gasping, and laboring up a slight incline a couple of miles from his home. Samantha had already disappeared over the brow of the hill and now she came back into sight jogging effortlessly. She came right up and started running around him in circles.

"C'mon, we've hardly started yet," she urged.

"Go and play with the traffic!" gasped Alex. She

grinned and linked her arm through his and almost dragged him up the rest of the hill. At the top he collapsed onto the pavement, his breath coming in great heaves. Samantha gazed down at him.

"You're so unfit it's unbelievable," she said.

"I'm all right," he grunted.

"You only do what you have to," she said. "C'mon, we'll walk a bit."

They walked down the other side of the hill, Alex still suffering. After a minute she cleared her throat and said casually, "That girl, Sue."

"What about her?" said Alex, surprised.

"You seem very good friends with her."

"She's a friend, yes," said Alex.

"A very close one, I'd say," said Samantha.

"So what?" demanded Alex. "Look, she's nearly eighteen — three years older than me, and she's engaged. She's not after me, I promise you."

"Oh, I didn't mean that," said Samantha hurriedly. "Alex, you can go out with who you like. I just thought it unusual, that's all."

"We've just known each other a while."

"C'mon, Alex, there's more to it than that."

He sighed. "You've got to promise not to laugh."

"Of course I won't laugh," she said sweetly.

"All right then," he said. "When I was in elementary school my mom used to pay her to walk me home."

Samantha let out a great shout of laughter. Alex

glared at her disapprovingly as she staggered around half doubled over with glee.

"I can see your word's really worth having," he said.

"Oh, that's wonderful," she gasped. "Did you use to hold her hand?"

"Don't push your luck," he said. Then added defensively: "There was a very busy road to cross." This only started her off again so he shut up until gradually she got herself back under control.

"I'm sorry, Alex," she said. "It just tickled me, that's all."

"Yes, well, you'd better not tell anybody," he said. "What did you want to know for, anyway?"

"Oh, no reason," she said. "C'mon, you must've got your breath back by this time, let's pick up the pace a bit."

"All right, but take it easy, will you?" he said. "If we turn right at the bottom of the hill it takes us back in the direction of my house."

"Oh, I don't know, Alex, I think we'd better find another way," said Samantha. She started to laugh again. "If we turn right there's a very busy road to cross."

# 9.
# Skating in Circles

Liz blew her whistle "OK, break it up every-one," she called to the Monday evening dance class. "You've half an hour to run through your medal dances."

"Good," said Samantha, grabbing for Alex's hand. "I was hoping she'd give us some space, tonight."

"You want any help, you two?" called Liz.

"No thanks, Liz," said Samantha, towing Alex into the middle of the ice.

"Not the Bronze dances again?" said Alex wear-ily.

"Actually, I thought we could try something different," she said. "I was running over some new steps Saturday night and I couldn't get them to work — I thought you might be able to help."

"Oh," said Alex, feeling pleased. "You mean there's something you can't do by yourself?"

"For the moment, yes," she said. "Now stop wasting time, will you? Look, I've been trying to dance in a tight circle but my feet keep getting away from me."

"You mean just skate in a circle?"

"No, dance! Sort of like this." She danced a high stepping trot around him but it didn't quite come off.

"Why?" he demanded.

"It's for our free dance."

"But we don't need it now."

"We'll need it one day," she said. "Anyway, can you see why I'm going off?"

"Your hips are in the wrong place, of course," he said. "You're doing it as a dance step not a skating step, with all your weight over the wrong leg — look, try it like this . . ." He skated a perfect tight circle around her. "Keep your weight over your standing leg and it'll lock it in position."

"Wait a minute." She stopped him.

"What?"

"I don't want her to see," said Samantha nodding to the sidelines. Maria Aitkiss was coming down the rubber steps carrying the huge dance cassette player she always used.

"Shall I go and tell her what we all think of her?" said Alex.

"I thought you were relieved?"

"I am! Believe you me!" said Alex. "It still doesn't make her any less of a cow, does it?" He heaved a sigh. "Oh, here we go." The cassette player burst into life with the music for Diane's free dance, loud enough to put everybody else off.

"Hi, Alex — Sam," said a voice.

"Sue," said Alex. "What are you doing here on a Monday?"

"You can never get enough practice," she said. Then she leaned forward and patted his hair into place, winked at him, and was gone in a quick flurry of ice. He turned back to Samantha, a fierce look on his face.

"Shut up!" he said.

"Right."

"I told you, we've known each other for years."

"Seems reasonable enough to me."

"And she just feels a bit responsible for me, that's all."

"Right."

"Oh, stop arguing," said Alex. "Anyway, you should be grateful to her, she's the one who started me skating in the first place."

"Did she?" said Samantha, surprised. "You mean she brought you along here?"

"In a way, yes," said Alex. He sighed. "Sometimes at night she used to look after me when my mom and dad went out. If it was on a skating night then she had to bring me along — I got interested watching, and that's it." He glared at her. She had an entirely innocent look on her face.

"I think baby-sitting is the word we're looking for here," she said.

"Right, that's it — you're dead!" said Alex, making a lunge for her.

"Aw, no, Alex — I won't tell, honest," she laughed, backing away. He frowned at her and she gave him the benefit of her best smile.

"C'mon, Diane's running through her program. Her mother won't notice us now," she said. "Let's try out those steps."

The next half an hour they went over the same few moves again and again, Samantha still finding it difficult. She kept relaxing back into her straight dancing whenever she lost concentration.

Again she tried and again her left foot refused to stay on track. She glanced at Alex, but he wasn't watching. He was standing, staring over at the sidelines.

"I'm sorry if I'm boring you," she said, cuttingly.

"There's something going on over there," he said nodding to where the rest of the dance class were gathered in a circle around Liz and Mrs. Aitkiss. Everybody seemed to be arguing. "Let's go and see what's happening."

"Oh, leave it, Alex," she said surprisingly. "It's nothing to do with us."

"I like a bit of gossip," he said. "And so, usually, do you."

"It's the first time the music's been off all night.

We've just got to run through the Bronze dances," Samantha said, taking a firm grip of his hand so that he was forced to follow.

Reluctantly, Alex let her bully him into the start position for the waltz.

He tried to skate while keeping the arguing crowd in view and was rewarded by sitting heavily down on the ice. He didn't get up for a minute. The meeting was breaking up now. Maria Aitkiss was storming off up the aisle and Diane was skating furiously across the ice toward them.

"I only hope you do that on your Bronze test," she spat out at the squatting figure of Alex, as she shot past.

"What was that for?" Alex said, getting to his feet.

"Oh, it's just her," said Samantha. "C'mon, it's time we called it a night."

They skated across to where Liz was packing up her kit. She looked up and gave them a smile.

"You've got your way then," she said.

"What d'you mean?" asked Alex.

"Mrs. Aitkiss has agreed to accept your entries," said Liz. "Providing you both get your Bronze medals, of course."

"Why?" Alex demanded. "She's not suddenly turned human, has she?"

"Because if she doesn't she won't have a competition," said Liz. "All the others said they'd withdraw if you weren't allowed in."

"All of them?" said Alex.

"Yes, even Nigel said he thought it wasn't fair — I shudder to think what Diane's going to do to him," said Liz.

Alex wasn't listening, he was staring at Samantha's innocent face with a dawning comprehension. He snapped his fingers at her.

"That's what Sunday was all about," he said. "You went around to Sue's, didn't you? Got her to arrange all this?"

"Me?" said Samantha, wide-eyed.

"Don't even try it," said Alex.

"Oh Alex, don't try to sweet-talk me," grinned Samantha. She turned to Liz. "So our names are down, are they?"

"Yep — so you'd better not fail your Bronzes now!" She picked up her sports bag and went off up the steps whistling to herself. Samantha turned back to find Alex glaring at her sternly.

"You'd better not open your mouth about me and Sue, that's all," he said.

She put her head on one side and said, "You don't really think I'd do that, do you?"

"I don't know anymore," said Alex. "All I know is that you go around manipulating people — well, you aren't going to do it with me! Understand?"

"Yes, Alex," she said meekly. "You're much too smart for that, anyway."

She glanced at her watch. "Look, I simply must rush. It'll be getting dark."

"Right," said Alex. He watched her skate off to the nearest exit, glad he'd got his own way at last. Slowly the smile on his face started to fade, as it gradually dawned on him.

"Wait a minute," he said to the empty rink. "I said I wasn't going to enter!"

Toby was battling with the vending machine in the cloakrooms when he heard the sound of raised voices. He gave the machine a kick. It had parted with a Mars bar but now it steadfastly refused to relinquish his change. The voices were getting louder and one of them was Alex's. So after a last thump, Toby abandoned his money and trundled off up the corridor.

"I'll get you later, pal!" he muttered over his shoulder at the piratical machine. Toby didn't exactly hurry but he quickened his steps in case he missed anything. When he rounded the corner he was so surprised that he stopped chewing his Mars bar.

Maxi Pearson, the captain of the ice hockey team, had Alex backed up against the lockers. Both of them were red-faced and were arguing in loud voices. Toby, not a boy easily disturbed, took another bite of his Mars bar and chewed it reflectively. This was unusual; Alex and Maxi had never gotten along. After a truly awesome fight back in the second year, Maxi had stayed well clear of Alex. "Get your hands off me," Alex said, pushing Maxi backwards. Toby winced. It looked like they were going to turn physical.

"I ought to belt you one," Maxi said.

"Don't push your luck," snarled Alex.

Maxi just looked at him, then turned and walked away in disgust. Alex glared after him.

"I take it you're off his Christmas card list from now on?" said Toby.

"Eh?" Alex turned on him. Then his expression relaxed when he saw who it was. "Oh yes. He's just made a very wise decision, to keep his mouth shut!" The last words were shouted after Maxi's retreating back.

"Hm." Toby finished off his Mars bar, examined the empty paper sadly, then stuffed it down the neck of a passing second year. "What were you discussing? The weather?" he said levelly.

"I just told him I'm quitting the hockey team."

Toby was jerked out of his nonchalance. "You're not serious?" he demanded.

"Afraid so," said Alex.

"You! Giving up hockey? You mean for ice dancing?"

"Keep your voice down, will you?" Alex glanced around the packed cloakroom, the meeting point for the seniors. "Toby, I had to. I can't do both! Not properly anyway."

"Well, that's easy. Give up the ice dancing."

"I can't." Alex ran his hand through his already ruffled hair. "Oh, I dunno, there seems to be more point to dancing than hockey — and to tell you the truth, I think I'm going to be better at it."

"How did Chris Macdonald take it?"

" 'Big Mac'? Very well, considering," said Alex. "He picked me up, slammed me against the wall, and told me he wouldn't let me back on the team if I crawled the length of the main street and kissed his foot — only he didn't say foot!"

"A kind of negative reaction then?" said Toby.

"I took it as one, yeah," said Alex.

"Well, I only hope you don't expect me to come and cheer you on at ice dancing," said Toby.

Alex looked blank. "Of course I do," he said.

"Well, you're going to be disappointed then."

"C'mon, Toby," said Alex. "Y'know I can't perform without you there."

"That once was enough," said Toby.

"Look, I'm sorry, Toby. I know you like watching the hockey, but ice dancing is getting important to me."

"Rubbish, it's that darn girl!"

"Samantha? Don't be stupid."

"Of course it is," sighed Toby. "The whole school knows about you two."

"They don't, do they?" Alex demanded.

"What do you think? There's been two dances in the last month and Alex Barnes, the terror of the dance floor, hasn't even put in an appearance," said Toby. Alex was shocked at the thought of the whole school knowing about his friendship with Samantha. He shook his head.

"No, I don't believe it," he said hopefully. "You're the only one who knows and you're not going to say anything." He prodded Toby in the chest aggressively. "I said, you're not gonna say anything!"

Toby grinned and pointed. "There's the cause of all the trouble." He raised his voice. "Hey Sammy, over here." Samantha, who was leaning against the wall talking to Roberta Isgrove, looked up and came over. Gradually she was being accepted by the others in the class as her reserve faded.

"I hope you realize you've ruined my Friday nights," Toby said seriously.

"Me? What have I done?" She said. Then she looked at Alex and smiled. "Do you want to borrow my comb?"

"No," he said, backing away, trying to stroke his hair back into place.

"What have I got to do with your Fridays?" she demanded of Toby.

"Everything! He's only gone and quit hockey so he can skate with you!"

"You haven't! Oh Alex!" Samantha was so pleased she gave him a quick hug, then, feeling that wasn't enough stood on tiptoe and kissed him. Immediately there was a loud cheer from everybody else in the cloakroom.

"Well, they all know now, don't they?" grinned Toby. "I'll leave you two lovebirds alone." He strolled away, before Alex could get hold of him. Everybody was watching them, so Alex grabbed hold of Samantha and dragged her round the corner.

"I could've done without you doing that," he said.

"Sorry," she said. "I couldn't help it. You've really given up hockey?"

"Did I have any choice?" he demanded. A group of grinning faces appeared round the corner and Alex headed for them, an angry look on his face. Samantha grabbed his arm.

"Leave them. They'll get over it," she said.

"I'm not sure I will," he said. "I'll never hear the last of it, y'know."

"I don't see that it matters," said Samantha. "You used to take girls to the school dances, didn't you?"

"Yes, but this is a bit different, isn't it? I mean I see you nearly every night of the week! Oh, never mind. Well, which is it going to be? Tuesday nights or sometime over the weekend?"

"Tuesdays are better. The weekends are too packed," she said. "I usually do an hour on a Saturday evening, but you can hardly move."

"So that means Mondays, Tuesdays, Wednesdays, and Thursdays?" he said. "All in a row?"

"You'll be starting later on Wednesday, remember, now that you no longer have hockey practice," she said.

"Well, I'm stuck for the words to express my gratitude," he said. "I'm telling you now, Samantha, four nights is it! You're not getting me to skate one minute longer than that."

"Of course not, Alex," she said her eyes wide with innocence. "I wouldn't dream of asking you to do any more. You don't know how grateful I am."

"Yeah?" he said. "OK then, I want you to answer me a question."

"What?"

"Why is it you let everyone call you Sam but me?"

"I don't."

"Yes, you do! Everybody calls you Sam: Liz, all the dance class, even Toby calls you Sammy."

She looked away. Her face flushed bright red. When she spoke, it was in a very small voice.

"You want the truth?"

"Well, it would make a nice change, yeah."

She forced herself to look into his eyes. "Anyone can call me Sam — most people do," she said. "But the people who matter to me, I like *them* to call me Samantha." She turned and almost ran away up the corridor.

Alex watched her go, a baffled look on his face. After a minute, he started to smile.

# 10.
# Thin Ice

The doctor unstrapped the blood-pressure cuff from Samantha's arm and put it back on his desk. He picked up a small flat stick and used it to push her tongue down, to study her throat.

"And how have you been feeling?" he asked.

"As long as people don't keep sticking bits of wood in me, I'm fine!" said Samantha.

"Samantha!" said her mother severely.

"Well, it's true," said Samantha sullenly. "This is all a waste of time. I'm perfectly all right."

It was Saturday morning a couple of months later, and Samantha was having her four-weekly checkup.

"I am sorry, doctor," said Mrs. Stephens.

"No, she's right," said the doctor. "She's as healthy as you or me."

"And her heart's all right?"

"As sound as a bell," said the doctor. Then to Samantha, "You are still taking the antibiotics?"

"Yes," she sighed. "I'm so full of pills, I rattle."

"Well, I'm afraid you must keep taking them for a few years yet," he said. "Apart from that, Mrs. Stephens, I think we can extend Samantha's checkups to every six months."

"Are you sure?" said Mrs. Stephens.

"Of course," said the doctor. Samantha almost smiled. She stood up, eager to go, but her mother hadn't quite finished.

"When do you think she could start joining in school sports, Doctor?" Mrs. Stephens asked. "I don't mean anything too strenuous, perhaps a bit of swimming?"

"She's strong enough now," said the doctor. "Anyway, it hardly applies, does it?"

"How do you mean?" asked Mrs. Stephens.

The doctor smiled. "I know all about this young lady," he said. "My wife's her skating coach, didn't you know? She was only talking last night about this medal test Samantha's taking this afternoon."

Doctor Pope parked his car outside the Stephens' house, left his bag inside, and went up the driveway. It was the same afternoon and he had just received an urgent call from Mr. Stephens. The front door was opened, before he had time to knock, and a worried-looking Mrs. Stephens showed him into the living room.

"Hello, Doctor, good of you to come," said Mr. Stephens coming forward to shake his hand.

"That's all right, Mr. Stephens — I take it you've had some trouble with Samantha?"

"We've just had the most awful scene with her, Doctor," said Mrs. Stephens. "Apparently she's been skating for months."

"Well yes, until this morning I presumed you knew."

"No we did not!" said Mr. Stephens. "We understood she was just going for walks each night to help her sleep."

"Doctor, you say you knew about the skating?" said Mrs. Stephens.

"I heard about it by chance some weeks ago."

"And you don't disapprove after what happened at dance school?" asked Mr. Stephens.

Doctor Pope sighed. "To be perfectly honest, she's probably doing more than I would strictly have advised," he said, "but with Samantha it's all or nothing, isn't it? After dance school she'd find it impossible to do anything halfheartedly."

"We nearly lost her last time," said Mrs. Stephens.

"I keep telling you, Mrs. Stephens, she's a normal, strong, healthy girl," said Doctor Pope. "If she has no recurrence it'll do her more good than harm."

"If there is no recurrence," repeated Mr. Stephens bleakly.

"But there is a chance of that, isn't there, Doctor?" said Mrs. Stephens.

"Statistically, it's possible. But if she carries on with the antibiotics she should be fine," said the doctor. "Anyway, I don't really see what else you can do. She'll never be happy if you stop her skating as well as dancing.

There was a silence for a moment. Mrs. Stephens heaved a sigh.

"You're right, of course. Now I think about it, it's obvious when she started skating — she stopped being moody and depressed."

"What triggered off this particular outburst?" asked Doctor Pope.

"I did, I'm afraid," said Mr. Stephens. "I got home at lunchtime and was confronted by all this. I naturally forbade her to skate again and was given a mouthful of abuse."

"Oh, it wasn't abuse, Donald," said Mrs. Stephens. "She was just upset, that's all. She was supposed to be doing this medal thing this afternoon and, of course, we stopped her."

"Yes, I know about the test," said Doctor Pope. He glanced at his watch and frowned, "She's too late now, it'll be half over — pity. Under the circumstances, it might have been better to let her take it."

"You wouldn't believe how she acted," said Mr. Stephens. "We had to send her to her room, Doctor. I mean, her mother literally had to drag her there! We've never had to treat Samantha like that."

"Perhaps I should have a word with her," said Doctor Pope, standing up. "What we need is to reach a compromise. Agree to her skating but keep a close eye on her."

Mrs. Stephens looked at her husband, who gave a shrug. "I'll go and get her," she said. Mrs. Stephens climbed the stairs.

"I think you've got to let her do something, Mr. Stephens," said the doctor.

"I'd rather do anything than go through another scene like today," said Mr. Stephens. "But I've got to admit, I'm still not happy."

"But is she happy?" said the doctor. "That's really what matters."

Mr. Stephens sighed, "I suppose so," he said. Both the men turned in surprise as Mrs. Stephens came down the stairs again.

"What's happened now?" asked Mr. Stephens. "Has she refused to come down?"

"In a way," said Mrs. Stephens. "She rather seems to have solved the problem about the medal test."

"What?" Mr. Stephens said, baffled. The doctor, more used to the ways of teenagers, gave a wry smile.

"The window." It wasn't a question.

"The window," Mrs. Stephens agreed. The doctor went to the door and opened it, then he looked back at the two worried parents.

"I only hope she passes after all this," he said.

# 11.
# Dramatic Gesture!

This time when Alex stepped off the ice, he knew he had passed. Samantha had made them practice so remorselessly that they had sailed through their three dances without a hitch. But for Alex that wasn't the main reason. Now he had a partner he could rely on. Whenever he was unsure of himself she was there, and he tried to do the same for her. The only bad time was during his solo when he felt very lonely out on the ice. When it was over, the realization hit him that he was made to be part of a skating partnership: not a hockey player, not an individual skater, but an ice dancer!

Samantha glowed as they received the brief smattering of applause when they were awarded their medals, but afterwards she seemed to go into a mood and disappeared toward the changing rooms without a word.

Alex was standing by the main doors when she

93

finally emerged. She had a sour look on her face, which grew even worse at the sight of the waiting Alex. She had hoped that he would have been gone by this time. He came straight over, all smiles, and tried to give her a hug.

"Do you mind?" she snapped.

"Pardon me for living," he said, hurt.

"I just don't feel like being touched at the moment."

"Oh, I thought that was allowed when we were in the rink," he said sarcastically. "Geez, Samantha, that's the whole point of what we do on the ice — touching each other."

"Well, we're not on the ice now!"

He shook his head, "C'mon, Samantha, loosen up, will you? We've just got our Bronze medals!"

"Forget the Bronze medals — leave me alone!" She slammed out of the glass doors into the falling darkness. Alex started after her, a blank look on his face.

He was a lot fitter these days but he didn't catch up with her until the end of the road.

"Samantha, wait," he gasped, panting for breath.

"I said leave me alone."

"I've got your medal." He grabbed her shoulder to stop her. "Look, here. You left it on the trainer's bench."

"You keep it."

"Oh, don't be so stupid!"

"Well, give it here then!" she said, snatching it from him. "If you don't want it then neither do I." She swung her hand. Alex jumped but he was too late and the medal went soaring out over the rooftops.

"There! Satisfied?" she said.

"You must be crazy."

"Yes, I must be," she said. "Now is that it? Can I go home now?

"Samantha!" He took her arm, a worried look on his face.

"No!" She knocked his arm aside. "What more do you want from me, Alex? You've got your medal, now get out of my life, will you!" She brushed past him but suddenly he grabbed hold of her and pushed her back against the fence that bordered the road.

"Ow — that hurt!"

"Good! Now you shut up and listen for once in your life!" Alex's face had gone white with anger. "You have got no right to treat me like this. No right! I have done everything you've asked of me: I skate virtually every night of my life, I've given up hockey. Hell, I even go for jogs with you on a Sunday instead of staying in bed — and I get this! Well, who needs it?"

Samantha had subsided, shocked by his outburst. She had never seen him really angry before. "I didn't . . ." she started.

"No! I don't want to hear it," he raged. "You

go boil your head, Samantha Stephens!" With an expression of disgust on his face, he turned away.

"My mother found out." She said, quietly, but even so it stopped him.

"What?"

"My mother found out about the skating."

"Oh." He stood looking at her, an exasperated look on his face, but now all the anger had gone. "Well, it wouldn't have hurt to tell me," he said at last. "What did she say?"

"What does it matter? I told you, that's it — end of story!" She turned to face the wooden fence and burst into tears. After a minute Alex's hands gently turned her back, and he held her while she cried.

"Why didn't you tell me?" he asked. She shook her head but didn't answer. "Oh, they won't stop you skating," he said.

"They stopped me dancing, didn't they?"

"We'll let it blow over a bit, then work something out," he said. "Skate weekends or something."

"It won't work, Alex." She dried her eyes on her sleeve. "We had a terrible fight this morning — I said some awful things! I told them I'd go on skating whatever they did!" She sniffed, then started to cry again. "They're going to send me away to boarding school."

"Look, stop crying, will you?" he sighed. "It's not the end of the world."

"Isn't it?" she said. "It's the end of *my* world, Alex! First dancing, now skating."

"But why! Why are they doing this?" he asked. "I've met your parents, they seem all right — they wouldn't do this without a reason."

"Have you really got to know?"

"Yeah, I think I have," he said. "I think you owe it me. It can't be anything that bad, surely?"

"It's not that, Alex," she said. "I just don't like telling people about it. They start treating me like an invalid." She sighed. "I got rheumatic fever very badly — I was ill for months. When I was over it my parents wouldn't let me go back to Tracy Powell's. They were right of course, it can affect your heart, you see. Once it's on your record, there isn't a dance school in the country who'll even look at you."

"But you're tons fitter than me," he protested.

"Yes, but once you've had it there's a faint chance of it recurring."

"So you're saying that's really it? It's all over!"

"Not for you," she said. "Alex, you don't think I wanted it this way, do you?"

"Why did you take the test at all if you knew you were finishing?" he said. "It's only got you into trouble."

She stared at him, then, "I couldn't let you down, idiot," she said.

"Oh, of course," he said, and there was an embarrassed silence between them before he said quietly, "You didn't have to buy the medal though, did you? The certificate's the thing that matters."

"I wanted to be a Bronze Medal skater even if only for a bit," she said. Then she gave a reluctant smile. "Besides, look at the dramatic gesture I got out of it — well worth the money."

"Yeah, I was very impressed," he said. "Look, Samantha, I'm sorry."

"So am I, so sorry," she said, wiping her eyes again. "Oh, what a pathetic scene — you must think me a real wimp."

"That's the last thing I'd think of you."

"Well, I suppose I'd better get back and face the music."

"Wait." He reached in his pocket, produced his medal and, before she could stop him, it followed hers out across the rooftops.

"What the . . .? Alex, don't be such a jerk!" she protested.

"I'm allowed a gesture too, aren't I?" he said. "Anyway, it's no good to me if you're quitting! What d'you expect me to do? Partner up with Diane again?"

Samantha was gazing at him. Suddenly she reached forward and gave him a hug. Then, embarrassed by the show of affection, she quickly released him again.

"C'mon," he said. "Let's get you home."

"You don't want to come home with me!" she said. "It's going to be a war zone back there!"

"We're still partners, aren't we?" he said as they started walking up the road together. After a minute she slipped her arm around his waist.

The house seemed very quiet when they got there. Samantha opened the door with her key and they crept inside. She looked at Alex and made a face.

"Here goes," she said, pushing open the door of the lounge. Mr. and Mrs. Stephens were sitting in the armchairs.

"Ah, Houdini returns," said Mr. Stephens, putting down his newspaper.

"I'm sorry," said Samantha quickly. "I had to go. You see, Alex hasn't practiced with anybody else."

"Hm — Alex, tell me, did you know that Samantha was skating without our knowledge?" asked Mr. Stephens.

"Yes, sir."

"Don't blame it on Alex. He didn't have any choice. I swore him to secrecy."

"I can well believe that," said Mr. Stephens. "Well, did you both pass?"

"Yes, thank you, Mr. Stephens," said Alex.

"Good, now stop looking so worried both of you and come and sit down," said Mrs. Stephens. They walked across the room and sat side by side on the sofa, but they still looked worried.

"We've had Doctor Pope here," said Mrs. Stephens.

"About me?" said Samantha in a small voice.

"Of course about you," said Mr. Stephens. "He is of the opinion that it would do you more harm than good, to try to stop you skating."

Samantha, who had been studying the toes of her sneakers, suddenly shot upright.

"You mean you're going to let me carry on?"

"Is there any way of stopping you?" said Mr. Stephens wryly.

"We think it's better if we know what you are doing so we can keep an eye on you," said Mrs. Stephens.

"I don't want you to think, Samantha, that we condone your behavior this afternoon," said Mr. Stephens, trying to play the heavy father.

"No, Daddy," she said trying to play the dutiful daughter, but her delight was showing through. "So, I can go on as normal then?"

"Now, not so fast," said Mr. Stephens. "You've been skating every night, is that right?"

Alex opened his mouth to speak, but Samantha got there first. "Yes, Daddy, seven nights a week — that'll be all right, won't it?"

"No, darling, that is too many," said Mrs. Stephens. "Apart from anything else it gives you no time for your homework."

"We think three nights is enough," said Mr. Stephens.

"Oh no, three nights isn't nearly enough," said

Samantha. "I'm sorry, but really it isn't! We're only on the ice for an hour and a half. If we're going to enter competitions, it's got to be every night!"

"Samantha, we're trying to be reasonable but you've got to meet us halfway," said Mrs. Stephens.

"Most of the other skaters practice mornings as well."

"There is no way we are going to agree to you skating seven nights a week," said Mr. Stephens sternly. There was a long silence, while Alex wished he was somewhere else.

Samantha said slowly, "I suppose we could try and manage on five."

Mrs. Stephens sighed and glanced at her husband, who gave a reluctant nod. "All right, we'll see how it goes," he said. "Five nights is an absolute maximum though — understand?" Samantha dashed across the room and gave him a hug. "But Alex, we want you to help us as well," said Mrs. Stephens. "If you think Samantha's overtired or doing too much, you're to make her stop immediately. Is that agreed?"

"Of course, Mrs. Stephens," said Alex, wondering how he was ever going to get Samantha to do something she didn't want to.

"Good, then that's settled," said Mrs. Stephens. "Alex, would you like to stay for tea?"

"Er, no, thank you very much, Mrs. Stephens, I'm late already," he said, standing up. "Thank you anyway."

Samantha showed Alex to the front door. He pulled her outside with him and lowered his voice.

"What was all that about?" he demanded. "The rink's closed on a Sunday anyway, and there's a hockey match every Friday night — you can only skate five nights a week as it is."

"Ssh," she said. "I'm just keeping them happy, that's all. I've been going out every night anyway. Now if I stay in two, they'll be pleased."

"You mean you asked for seven because you knew they'd agree to five?"

She looked sheepish. "I like to let my dad think he's still running things," she admitted. Alex laughed and went up the pathway.

"Alex?" Her call stopped him, she came up the path after him. "Thanks for coming home with me." She reached up and gave him a kiss.

"That's OK, Samantha," he said. "You just made it all worth it."

# 12.
# Homework

On the following evening Samantha was lying on her bed, working away in her sketch pad. The Torvill and Dean poster now had achieved pride of place and poor Mikhail Baryshnikov had been relegated to the position behind the door. Samantha heard a footstep on the landing and hurriedly slid a math folder on top of the sketch pad. Her mother came into the room.

"Not going out for a walk tonight then, darling?" said Mrs. Stephens.

"I thought I'd better get on top of my homework," said Samantha.

"Hm." Her mother sat on the side of the bed, reached across, and pulled the sketch pad out from under the math folder. Samantha turned bright red.

"I've got to put the finishing touches to this free dance," said Samantha defensively. "We've only a month left."

"Isn't that your coach's job?"

"I don't want her to do it."

"Why not!"

"Because — because, well, I think I can do it better," said Samantha. "Anyway, I don't want any of the other skaters to see it before the night of the competition."

"Darling, I know you're well trained in dance, but this is skating!"

"That's the point they are all missing. It's the same!" Samantha said, sitting up in her excitement. "Sure, you've got to fit the skating steps into it, and the whole thing's faster, but their idea of a free dance at our level is just to string a few moves together. They don't try and tell a story! They don't even have a theme!"

"And you intend to just spring this on them?"

"I don't want anybody to realize that we're in with a chance to win."

"But you've got to practice it, surely?"

"We've been doing that for months, little bits here and there, and there's hardly ever anybody there on Thursdays," said Samantha. She gave a secret smile. "Anyway, I've got an idea about that."

"I'm sure you have," said her mother. She studied her eager daughter anxiously. Samantha seemed as happy now as when she had been at dance school. Mrs. Stephens hoped she wasn't going to fall flat on her face over this free dance idea. "And this ice dancing is really what you want to do, is it?"

"Oh yes!" said Samantha. "It's, it's . . . oh, I don't know, more exciting, freer, more dangerous than dancing!"

"Well, yes, you can hardly win an Olympic Medal for dance, can you?" said her mother. "You're not going to get too involved with it, are you? You know what your father said?"

"Yeah."

"Don't say yeah, darling — I hope that's not the influence of that boy."

"That's not fair, I've always said yeah," said Samantha. "I thought you liked Alex?"

"I do, just as long as you don't get too fond of him," said her mother. She tapped the math folder. "And remember what you promised about your schoolwork?"

"I'm doing a lot better lately. I came top in graphic design!"

"Really," said her mother. "What did you have to design?"

"Oh, nothing much. We could choose."

"Yes?" Her mother raised her eyebrows.

"A dance costume," Samantha admitted. Her mother had to laugh despite herself.

"You know your father's still very annoyed with you?"

"Yes." Samantha lowered her eyes and tried to

look meek. Then after a decent pause, "Mommy, do you think he'd consider buying us costumes for the free dance?"

"Well, you've really got nerve" said Mrs. Stephens.

"I've got to have costumes, you see," said Samantha. "And Alex's mom and dad wouldn't pay for his even if he asked."

Mrs. Stephens got to her feet and went to the door, shaking her head, half in disbelief, half in amusement.

"Shall I come down and ask him now?" said Samantha.

"No, darling," said her mother. "I would leave it a few days, if I were you."

It was the following Friday. After four days the crowd of spectators around the gym windows had faded away. Now, there were only three first-year girls left, with their noses pressed up against the glass.

Alex was standing, staring at Samantha in horrified amazement.

"You want me to wear what?" he demanded.

"Please, Alex, it'll look great," said Samantha.

"Look, Samantha, I've given up hockey. I'm skating just about every night of my life. I'm doing push-ups every morning till my arms feel like they're about to drop off — I've even made a fool of myself in front of the whole school by jumping around in the gym every lunchtime! But I am *not* going to get dressed up like, like, like . . ." his voice trailed away.

"My dad's paying for it," said Samantha. "You can't go disappointing him after all he's done."

"But . . ." Alex broke off, baffled by her reasoning. "Anyway, everybody else will be wearing normal skating outfits."

"Exactly." There was a long pause while Alex ran his fingers through his hair and Samantha gazed at him, with an innocent look on her face. "How many can you do then?" she said at last. "Push-ups, that is?"

"Eh? Oh, seventy-two."

"That's great, isn't it?"

"Don't try and change the subject. I'm not agreeing to this — no way," he said. "Anyway, it wouldn't work. I'd trip over it."

"Nah! You're much too good a skater. You never fall over," she said sweetly.

"Oh, don't give me your soft soap," said Alex. "You just stick to the normal Samantha: abrasive, domineering, unreasonable! I'm used to all that."

"OK," she said brightly. "If you don't do it, I'll tell everybody how your mother calls you Honey Bunch."

"You would too, wouldn't you?" said Alex aghast. "I knew I shouldn't have had you back to tea."

"Honey Bunch Barnes," mused Samantha.

"Just think of it. The whole school will be using it by the end of the week."

"I'll do it," said Alex hastily. He thought for a moment. "But Sam . . . Samantha, we've got to try skating in full costume before the night."

"I've got that arranged," she said. "We should have the costumes by next weekend and my dad will run us over to the rink at Richmond, on Saturday, and we can skate all afternoon."

"All dressed up you mean?" demanded Alex. "They'll think we've escaped from a lunatic asylum."

"Yeah, I suppose they will," said Samantha, "But the important point is, that this is a club competition and nobody at Richmond will be entering."

Alex sighed. "Does it have to be a Saturday afternoon? It'll be packed!"

"Well yes, we have to go to the new Andrew Lloyd-Webber rock opera the same evening," she said. "I thought it'd be best to get it all done on the same day."

"You mean you and your parents are going to the rock opera thing?"

"No, you and me of course."

"Why me?"

"Because the music we're dancing to is the theme song from the show," she said.

"And you've arranged all this before you thought of discussing it with me?"

"Yeah," she said. "I knew you'd agree." She held out her hands to him. "C'mon, there's time to run through it a couple of more times before we have to go back to class."

Warily Alex took her in his arms and they clumped off up the wooden floor, finding it slow and too safe after the ice. Alex wasn't concentrating as much as usual. He still had a worried look on his face. Samantha guided him through the routine, until they came to their middle section, then she stopped and shook him back to reality.

"This bit here," she said. "I've been thinking. Would it work with me on my knees?"

"Eh? Oh, you mean when I swing you round in a circle!"

"Yeah, it'd look great."

"Hm, it would — there's a problem with it though, Samantha," he said, biting his bottom lip in thought. "You wouldn't make it all the way round. There's too much traction."

"I gave it a try on Wednesday night and it didn't seem that much different," she said.

"When did you try it? Before the lesson started?"

"Yes, before anybody else was there."

"You mean right after the hockey match when the ice had just been resurfaced?" he said. "Look, Samantha, it'd work OK if we could guarantee to be the first on, but once the ice has been cut up

by the others it's covered with a fine layer of snow.
It slows you right down — it won't work."

"Oh, OK . . . just a thought," she said. They
started off again, Alex trying to imagine how the
dance would work when they were both wearing
costumes.

After a moment Samantha brought him to a
stop. "Something's bothering you, Alex."

"No — I'm all right," he said.

"What is it?" she demanded.

"Well, it's these costumes and the rest of the
stuff," he said. "You say your dad's paying for it
all?"

"Of course."

"But I can't let him do that."

"Oh, don't worry about it — he offered," said
Samantha.

"And he's prepared to give up his entire Saturday afternoon driving us all over London?"

"The evening as well. He won't let me come
home that late at night on my own."

"And he doesn't mind?" said Alex.

"Course not!" said Samantha. She started him
off dancing again and they rounded the end of the
gym, just missing the wall bars. His eyes met
hers, and she gave her small smile. "Anyway, he
won't when I ask him," she said.

# 13.
# The School Dance

On the Saturday night before the competition nearly everyone who was entering turned up to practice, in spite of the crush of people. Samantha was skating around on her own trying to get her speed up.

She skidded around the end of the center space and skidded to a stop to avoid a young girl, who was sitting on the ice laughing.

"Whoops, I can't get up," grinned the girl.

"Why can't you stay round the edge where you belong?" snapped Samantha. "The center's for people who can skate!"

"Sorry," said the girl, embarrassed. She scrambled to her feet and lurched off back to the barriers.

"Darn!" said Samantha to herself. She watched the other girl for a minute then went after her and tapped her on the shoulder.

"Look, it's me that should be sorry," said Samantha. "I had no right to say that."

"Oh — er, no, that's OK," said the girl. "I should have kept out of your way."

"You have as much right to be here as anyone," said Samantha. "It's me, I'm sorry. I'm in a bad mood about something, that's all."

"Oh," said the girl, visibly cheering up. "I was watching you skate. That's why I was in the center — I think you're brilliant."

"Ha — if only I was," said Samantha. "Look, I'm in a competition next week. When that's over, if you'd like me to help you with a few basics then I'd be glad to."

"That'd be great," said the girl. "Will you have time?"

"I'll make time," said Samantha. "I'll look for you — OK?"

"Thanks," said the girl. She looked after Samantha as she skated away. Samantha went off the ice to stretch. She eased herself into the full side split position, ignoring the envious glances of the other skaters.

Samantha didn't need to stretch. She'd already done that once in the changing rooms, but she knew if she didn't get her mood under control her skating would suffer. She took a very deep breath and exhaled it slowly, easing her feet apart another painful inch.

She and Alex skated four nights a week religiously and she didn't really mind spending one lonely night on the ice. It gave her a chance to hone her skating skills. Alex usually went out with Toby on a Saturday but that night was the monthly school dance and she had heard two of the other girls from her class giggling about how Roberta Isgrove had finally agreed to go with him after years of asking. Not that she minded of course, she told herself savagely. Alex was perfectly entitled to go out with any girl he wanted to!

"Showing off again?" said a voice. She looked up. Diane was standing at the very edge of the ice, a sour look on her face. Samantha sighed and eased her feet in. Stretching was a good way to change her mood but often an argument could have the same effect.

"You do enough of that for both of us," said Samantha.

"Why don't you go back to your precious dance school?" said Diane, probing Samantha's weakness.

"Because I prefer skating."

"Pity you can't skate then, isn't it?"

"Hm," mused Samantha. "Look, you've got ice all over you where you fell down." She pointed.

"I suppose you never fall down?"

"Only when people bang into me."

"I should watch yourself if I were you. It could happen again!"

Samantha shrugged. "I can give you some help if you want."

"What?" Diane had an incredulous look on her face.

"You're falling down so much because you're getting dizzy," said Samantha. "You're moving your head wrongly when you spin: You've got to learn to 'spot' your gaze."

"*You* are trying to tell *me* how to skate?" Diane's voice rose to a shout.

"No, I'm trying to tell you how to *dance*," said Samantha. "Somebody's got to."

"You arrogant . . . I was skating before you had your first bra!"

"At least I need one," said Samantha.

"Diane, what is this?" said Mrs. Aitkiss, coming over to see what was going on.

"It's this girl here, Mother," said Diane. "She's trying to give me some advice about my skating."

"Ah, yes, it's Samantha Stephens, is that right?" said Mrs. Aitkiss.

"Fame at last," said Samantha.

"Well, Samantha, I can assure you that I am able to coach my daughter without your — er, shall we say, valuable assistance?"

"Yeah?" said Samantha. "I was only saying that if she was going to spend that much time sitting on the ice, she should bring a chair."

Mrs. Aitkiss blinked, then she waved a hand at her daughter. "Diane, go and find Nigel. He should be warmed up by this time. Then, run through that sequence again." She waited until

114

Diane was out of earshot before she turned back to Samantha. "Now you listen to me, young lady, I have got a great deal of influence with the dance club here."

"Wow — I'm impressed!" said Samantha. Mrs. Aitkiss breathed heavily.

"You've bulldozed your way into my — this competition," she said coldly. "The dance club's on show. If you make us look bad in anyway, I'll make sure you never skate here again."

Samantha stifled a yawn and stepped back onto the ice. She skated back to the center, feeling lonely. Then all at once things started to look better. Alex was skating towards her, an inane grin on his face.

"What are you doing here?" she demanded.

"C'mon, it's only a week to the competition," he said. "I do have some sense of responsibility, you know."

"I thought you were going to the school dance?" she said.

"I knew it!" he said. "When you weren't around my house this morning, dragging me out for a training run, I knew you'd found out about me taking Bobby Isgrove to the dance."

She shrugged. "You can go out with who you like."

"Too right I can!" He was laughing at her. "Look, it's just a joke between me and Bobby. I've been asking her out since the sixth grade.

This time she took the joke a bit further and accepted — that's all."

"So what have you done with her?"

"I'm hoping she really has got a good sense of humor — I'm afraid I've dumped her," he said. "It could well be the end of what might have been a beautiful relationship."

"Oh." She took his hands and steered him around the ice. "It's just that we need to skate, Alex. We've only got a few more days."

"That's why I'm here," he said blandly.

She risked a glimpse at him. He was still laughing. She gave him a shake. "Look, I'm glad you're here — right? End of story!"

"Fine," he said. "Anyway, I'm not guaranteeing to skate every Saturday."

"That's all right. I don't expect you to, Alex," she said. "You won't want to anyway, when we're skating early mornings next year." He was just starting on a horrified reply when a speeding figure loomed into view. Samantha pushed Alex backwards out of the way then executed a beautiful turn around Diane, who managed to trip over Samantha's skate. She went down with a crash.

"Sitting down again, Diane?" said Samantha sweetly.

"Jerk!" snarled Diane.

"You talking about me, or your mother?" called Samantha, skating away with Alex.

"I take it you've won another round with 'Desperate Diane' " said Alex.

"Me?" she said wide-eyed.

"What did you say to her this time?"

"Actually, I was trying to help — don't look at me like that, Alex, seriously I was!" said Samantha. "I was telling her how to stop getting dizzy when she turns."

"Well, I only wish you'd show me."

"I would have, but you don't seem to need it."

"I'll tell you straight, Samantha," he said. "The last fifteen seconds of our free. You know when we're doing all that dancing around the pole bit? I can hardly stay on my feet!"

"You never told me that."

"I didn't think there was anything I could do about it."

"Of course there is! How d'you think jazz dancers manage?" She stopped and turned him to face the clock at the far end of the rink. "Now let your body turn but keep your eyes on the clock."

"I'll break my neck!"

"No, it's much too thick for that. When you've gone as far as you can, turn your head quickly all in one go till you're facing the clock again."

He tried, failed, tried again and then again, until he was starting to get it.

"Hey, that's not so bad," he said.

"Yeah, I don't think it will work for those fast

spins they do in solo skating but when we just have to turn quickly, it's fine," she said. "Only you have to practice until it becomes automatic. Dancers call it 'Spotting.' You'll find you won't get nearly as dizzy."

"We'd better try and fit it into our free," said Alex. "I don't want to end up on my bottom."

"You mean now?" said Samantha. "Everybody's here."

"Samantha, we've got to! We've hardly skated the whole thing yet," he said. "Anyway, what's it matter if the others see it?"

"It matters because it's better than theirs," said Samantha. "And I don't want them to find that out! I especially don't want Diane to find that out."

"Aw — c'mon," said Alex. "She's so busy she won't notice — anyway we haven't got the music or the costumes. It won't mean anything to her."

Reluctantly Samantha took his hands and they started to skate.

# 14.
# The Competition

Look at all those people," said Alex, in a worried voice.

"Just concentrate on the music," said Samantha. "Once you start skating you won't actually notice the crowd at all."

"I take it you've danced in front of people lots of times?"

"A few," said Samantha. Then she added quietly, "It doesn't get any easier."

It was the Saturday afternoon of the competition and Alex had never seen so many people at the rink. Samantha's parents were somewhere in the crowd, but Alex had been so embarrassed at the thought of competing that his family didn't even know about it.

Samantha and Alex were hiding in the mouth of the tunnel, watching Diane and Nigel skate their compulsory dances. They were just coming to the end of their third circuit and the music faded, taking them to the edge of the ice.

Samantha dragged Alex back out of sight so Diane wouldn't see them watching. He pulled a face.

"They're better than us," he said.

"They're different, that's all — more regimental," she said.

"Better is what they are!" said Alex. He leaned against the wall and slid down it until he was sitting on the rubber floor. Samantha looked at him in exasperation for a minute, then she gave a sigh and went and joined him. They were the last on and had to sit listening to the others' music for what seemed to be hours.

The Maria Aitkiss competition was a club event and, as such, wasn't recognized by the International Skating Union, so Diane's mother had been free to set her own rules. The couples had to skate two compulsory dances from the junior tests and Alex and Samantha had chosen the foxtrot and fourteen-step from the Bronze.

Finally, their names were called and Samantha pulled Alex to his feet and they skated out onto the ice.

The foxtrot went well, the best it had ever gone for them. As Samantha had said, once Alex started skating, he didn't notice the crowd. The fourteen-step didn't go as smoothly. The other seven couples had churned up the ice a good bit and, on their second circuit, Samantha hit a ridge and would have gone over if Alex hadn't caught her in time. Even so, it upset their rhythm and although Samantha immediately settled back into their routine, Alex couldn't. They came to a ragged halt and the crowd gave them some brief, polite, applause. Everybody was waiting for the free dances, bored by the repetitious compulsories. Only a loyal Toby was making a lot of noise, pretending to be enthusiastic.

Samantha viewed their marks with disgust and she wouldn't speak until they were back in the anteroom. She dragged Alex behind the lockers.

"Fourth place," she said crossly. "I don't know what you're looking so pleased about."

"I'm looking pleased because I didn't think we'd do nearly as well as that," he said.

"Look, we've got to make up three places if we're going to win!"

"Oh, don't be so crazy!" Alex gave a genuine laugh of surprise. "It's a miracle we've gotten this far."

"Are you seriously telling me you didn't enter this to try and win?" she demanded.

"Of course we're not going to win," he said. "C'mon, Samantha, be realistic. Diane and Nigel are going to win. They're miles ahead already! We could have a shot at third if you want." Just then Liz came into the room and clapped her hands.

"Thirty minutes, everybody, while they resurface the ice," she called.

"What's the order of the free dance?" asked Melanie.

"Same order."

"I thought they reversed it, so the leaders went last?" said Barry.

"That's what they usually do, isn't it, Liz?" asked Jason.

"Mrs. Aitkiss wants it the same order," said Liz. Everybody automatically looked at Diane, who shrugged.

"Mother wants everybody to have as long as possible between the compulsories and free," she said.

"Nothing to do with the ice not being churned up for her precious daughter," muttered Alex. Samantha didn't say anything. She sat down and started to unlace her skates. Alex watched her for a minute, then he did the same.

"You going to have a word with your parents?" he asked.

"I am not!" she said. "The last thing I need at this moment is a lecture on working too hard — I thought I'd go and get a little air."

"I'll come with you."

"No!" she said, a bit sharply. "I'm sorry, I'd like to be on my own for a while." She studied him for a minute, leaned forward, and patted his hair down flat. "Alex, look, thanks for being my partner," she said. "I know I'm bossy, but you've

been really great! You've fitted in with everything: the extra nights skating, the school gym,
the jogging on Saturday and Sunday mornings
when you wanted to stay in bed — you even gave
up your hockey."

"You didn't give me much choice," he grinned.

"No, I'm sorry," she said. "Maybe after today
we should think about a change."

"What? You mean a change of partner?"

"Well, yes. I'm too pushy for you, Alex. You
want to be free to do other things — hang out,
play hockey, stuff like that."

"I don't want another partner, Samantha!"

"I'm sorry, Alex, but *I* do."

He looked hurt. "Why? Just because I don't
think we can win?"

"That's part of it." She leaned forward and
touched his knee. "Look, I don't want to hurt your
feelings, but I told you, Alex, I can't treat skating
as a hobby."

"That's good, that is," he said. "You're only
doing this because you're not allowed to dance."

"You want the truth?"

"Not if it's going to hurt!"

"That *was* the reason at first," she admitted. "I
looked down on ice dancing — but not anymore!
I wouldn't go back to straight dance now if I could.
The ice gives you a freedom, a speed, a — oh, I
don't know, I can't explain it." She gave her half-

smile. "Anyway, dancers are usually just backing acts for a singer. In ice dancing, for that three or four minutes, you're the star!"

"And you don't think I can be a star?" he said quietly.

"Oh yes, that's why I chose you for a partner."

"You chose me?"

"Of course I did," she said. "I arranged it all with Liz — you're the only person in the dance club who could be a star if he wanted." She put her skates in her locker and latched the door. "And that's the problem, Alex — you don't want to, do you?"

Alex sat drinking a soda in the cafeteria and watching Toby eat a huge plate of food.

"Toby, how many push-ups can you do?" he asked.

"Eh — push-ups?" said Toby. "None."

"Have you tried?"

"Alex, a push-up is a thing I know I can't do without even trying," said Toby. "I'll tell you what I can do though, I can make a better apple pie than this."

"Well, ask me how many I can do."

"Go on then."

"One hundred and one."

"I'm so pleased for you," said Toby. He prodded the pie on his plate with his fork. "Pastry's like reinforced concrete," he muttered. The PA burst into life and an unintelligible noise came out.

Toby looked up. "What was all that about?"

"It was warning us that we've only got ten minutes," said Alex, getting to his feet.

"You mean to say you understood that racket?"

"Years of practice," said Alex. "You coming? I need at least five minutes to get into my costume."

"Er, in a minute," said Toby. "I've got to have my dessert yet. You're on last, aren't you?"

"Yep."

"Well, I'll be there for yours, don't you worry," said Toby with a sigh. He went back to his pie. Alex grinned and hurried off to the changing room.

Ten minutes later he slid in at the back of the anteroom feeling very self-conscious in his costume. He was relieved to find that Samantha was the only one still there. She gave him a smile.

"I thought you might have abandoned me," she said.

"No, you didn't!" he said.

"No, I didn't," she agreed. She stood up to test her skates. Alex was putting his on with the ease of long practice. When he was ready, she looked him up and down.

"You look really great," she said.

"What about my hair?"

"You can't see it, dodo," she smiled. "How about me?"

"You always look good," said Alex, surprisingly. "Is everybody else warming up?"

"Well, more having a bit of practice I think."

"We'd better get down, hadn't we?"

"Yeah," she said. "Look, Alex, what we were talking about earlier — let's just do our best tonight, eh?"

"That's what I was intending to do all along."

When they reached the ice the other skaters were gliding around the rink and the crowd was only just pushing back to their seats. Alex didn't look for Toby. He knew he wouldn't show his face until the last moment. They could feel the other skaters' eyes on them. Only Liz knew about their costumes and, out of the others, only Diane and Nigel were wearing anything that resembled an original outfit: ordinary skating costumes with oriental designs on them in keeping with their music.

"The thing is to act cool," said Samantha, stepping onto the ice. "Pretend we always dress like this."

Alex took a deep breath and followed her, but the minute he pushed himself off there was a loud screeching noise.

"What the . . .?" he said. He tried again. The ice dragged at his skates. He lifted a foot to study the blade.

"Is there any ice on the edge?" he asked Samantha. She had a look but there was nothing, so he tried again and the same thing happened. Worried, they rushed back to the anteroom and he unlaced his skates. Liz saw them go and followed them.

"What's wrong?" she asked. Alex was studying the bottom of his blades.

He sighed. "Someone's been messing around with my skates," he said, holding them out to her. She glanced at them, then studied them more closely.

"Someone's taken the edge off," she said. "Rubbed a bit of stone over them or something — where did you leave them?"

"In here, on top of the lockers — I thought they'd be safe."

"They should've been. Only skaters and coaches are allowed in here," said Liz.

"Exactly," said Samantha.

"What's that supposed to mean?" demanded Liz.

"It means Diane was in here," said Samantha.

"Oh, c'mon, Samantha. You can't go around making accusations like that," said Liz.

"Well, what do you think, Alex?" asked Samantha. He shrugged and wouldn't answer.

"See, he thinks it was her, too," said Samantha.

"What about yours?" asked Liz. "Are they all right?"

"Yes, mine were locked up," said Samantha

pointedly. Liz thought for a moment then shook her head.

"I can't see it," she said. "Just to spite you?"

"Oh no, that's not the reason," said Samantha. "She saw our free last Saturday — she knows we can win with it."

Liz was silent while she had another think. From the look on her face Samantha and Alex could tell she believed them.

"Well, what do you want me to do about it?" she said after a minute. "I can't just go out there and accuse her! You haven't got any proof, have you?"

"No, but we know," said Samantha bitterly. "Darn, after all that work she's going to get away with it."

"No she isn't!" said Alex speaking for the first time. The others stared at him in surprise. His face was bone-white. For the second time Samantha was seeing him really angry. "I'll borrow some skates from the booth."

"You can't compete in hired skates!" protested Liz.

"I can!" said Alex. "I'll compete in bare feet if necessary; she's not getting away with this!"

"They're not even dance blades," said Liz.

"I'm an ex-hockey player, I can skate in anything." He made for the door, then stopped and looked back at Samantha. His gaze softened.

"Don't panic," he said. "She's got my back up this time — now we're going to win."

Liz looked at Samantha, who was giving her half-smile. "What was that all about?" Liz asked.

"Nothing much," said Samantha. "It's just that I think I've got a real partner at last!"

# 15.
# Apache

Never had the rink looked so vast, so lonely. The announcer had just read out their names, so now there was no escape. They were really going to have to go out there in front of all those people! Alex took a deep breath. Samantha grabbed his hand and they glided the thousand miles to the center of the ice.

Diane and Nigel had performed a free dance that had kept them in first place but hadn't improved their lead. Alex, watching it, his enthusiasm still fired up by his anger, now felt more confident. Diane and Nigel's free dance lacked flair and style and, though it might have been technically good, it was also boring. Whatever the crowd thought about the dance Samantha had choreographed, it was unlikely to bore them.

Lisa and Barry had improved to second place. Jason and Claire had managed to get tangled up and had both fallen — a thing Alex hadn't seen before. Jason had been so upset that they had retired.

Third place was still being held by Melanie and Larry but they had only been half a point ahead of Alex and Samantha after the compulsories.

Alex could feel the crowd staring and craning forward to view their costumes better. He was dressed as an Indian chief with jerkin and canvas trousers. On his head he wore the full feather headdress that stretched right down his back. Samantha was dressed as a squaw, more simply but more attractively, with just a single feather in her headband.

The announcer read their names out again and Alex gulped, wondering if anybody had actually passed out on the ice before. He glanced nervously around at the forest of eyes watching him. Samantha jerked his arm roughly.

"Look at me!" she said sharply. "Forget them — they don't matter. Just look at me!" He stared into her eyes and, suddenly, he realized that she was as terrified as he was. He gave her hand a reassuring squeeze.

"Easy!" he said.

*Bang!* Their music had started, the rhythmic drumbeat coming over the main speakers louder than they had ever heard it before. Alex felt Samantha jump when the music came, but then she relaxed as they waited for the third bar that would move them.

All the other skaters had chosen serious music to start with, changing to faster music in the middle and usually ending up with a dramatic flourish. Samantha had designed a dance around the title song of Andrew Lloyd-Webber's *Apache*, the instrumental that had topped the charts for the last month. It lasted almost exactly three minutes and they danced the whole record without a single change.

At last the third beat arrived and they moved off, almost slowly, with snakelike, sinuous movements as though stalking one another, Alex the tracker, Samantha running around him. Gradually the music speeded up, taking the two skaters with it and now they were hunting the whole ice as if it were the empty plains of the Apache tribes.

Alex hardly noticed his skates, he just had to take a little more care on the sharp turns, because they didn't hold the ice quite as well, but Samantha had remembered and was making allowances in her skating.

Samantha was feeling happy, the dance was going well, the costumes felt good and looked good. She'd been worried about Alex's headdress, whether it would stay in place or get tangled up, but it flowed out behind him when he turned, making it even more effective than she had planned. The dance went on, the three minutes seeming to stretch out before them forever. Then, almost suddenly, they were into the last half-minute and they had reached the bit she had had so much trouble with, where they danced round an imaginary totem pole: The short sharp steps of a war dance.

Finally they turned to face a huge yellow spotlight, set up to simulate the sun. Side by side they glided towards it, arms outstretched as they entreated it to return. She sighed with relief as their music began to die away, but it changed to a gasp of horror because Alex had forgotten about his skates. Forgotten they didn't grip the ice like his normal skates. With a lurch, he toppled forward completely off balance — and the ex-hockey player in him took over so that he relaxed into the fall and sank to his knees, making the ending twice as effective. And Samantha had the quickness of wit to sink to her knees alongside him, only a second behind, so the whole thing looked planned.

They grinned with relief at each other. Everyone was applauding. They held the pose for another second before Alex helped her up and, instead of bowing, they held their hands high in the traditional greeting of the Indian as they returned to the sidelines.

Some of the most enthusiastic applause was coming from the dance club members in the front rows. Liz wasn't applauding, just beaming. Even Nigel was clapping enthusiastically, an empty seat at his side where Diane had abandoned him.

They stopped at the entrance to the tunnel and Samantha gave him a nudge with her elbow.

"We haven't really discussed this early morning skating yet," she said.

"Eh?" he said, staring indignantly at her. Then he grinned and put an arm round her. "I'll tell you straight, Samantha, I'm not doing more than one morning a week!"

A sudden yell from where Toby was sitting told them that their marks had gone up. Samantha studied them with grudging satisfaction, Alex with delight. Toby was standing on his seat bawling his head off and showering everybody with popcorn.

"Y'know," said Alex conversationally, "I think old Toby's quite getting to like ice dancing."

# About the Author

Nicholas Walker was born in the United Kingdom and has managed to do quite a few interesting things. Mr. Walker studied law and banking. He ran clubs and hotels — he even ran a restaurant when he was only twenty-one! At present, he runs a karate club, but spends his free time cycling, parachuting, ice skating, and writing.

Mr. Walker lives with his wife and two children in Penzance, England.

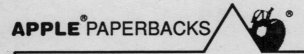